The Royal Diaries

CLEOPATRA VII

DAUGHTER OF THE NILE

BY KRISTIANA GREGORY

Scholastic Inc.
New York Toronto London Auckland Sydney
Mexico City New Delhi Hong Kong Buenos Aires

SCROLLS I–7
57 B.C.

3 JANUARIUS, MORNING

I, Cleopatra, Princess of the Nile, write this in my own hand.

Many rooms in the palace are mine, but this small one at the northeast corner is my favorite. It overlooks the sea. Waves beat wildly against the shore for another storm is upon us, our fifth this winter. The clouds are dark. Even wrapped in my chiton, I feel cold.

It is most urgent that I record the troubling events of this week. Father has gone into hiding, having fled for his life. Though it is the twenty-third year of his reign, he is in danger of losing his throne. He is, of course, King Ptolemy Auletes, honored pharaoh of Egypt.

Three nights ago while Father slept, a deadly puff adder was found curled at the foot of his bed, ready to strike. Father's old eunuch Mento, who sleeps on the floor next to him, was awakened by a hiss. He threw himself on the snake and tried to strangle it, but was bitten on the wrist. He died in torment a few minutes later. Father watched the snake slide off the bed and across the marble floor. As I write this, it has not been caught.

An accident? *Perhaps*, thought Father. Until today.

Because he mourns Mento, his beloved slave since boyhood, Father has refused comfort. When wine was brought to him this morning, with hopes it would make his heart merry, the royal cupbearer seemed nervous, for as he held out the tray the goblet rattled.

"Why are you shaking?" Father demanded. When the man did not answer, Father angrily motioned for the cupbearer to take the first sip, quickly, which he did.

I was standing behind a column, watching. When the goblet and silver tray fell to the floor, the crash echoed through the wide hall. I covered my mouth to silence my scream, but still guards came running.

The cupbearer lay in the puddle of wine, writhing in the agony meant for my father. Moments later he was dead. The poison was probably from the *eto* plant. It is as swift and deadly as a snake's.

To continue . . .

Where Father has hidden and with whom, I do not know. His suite of rooms has been taken over by my eldest sister, Tryphaena, who has long admired the sweeping view of the sea from his balcony. Father's servants do not argue with her because she is as snappish and cold-eyed as a crocodile.

I do not trust Tryphaena. She wants to be queen and has mocked our father for being a poor leader, though how she became an expert on leadership I cannot guess. When I visited her late this afternoon, she was soaking in the heated pool that is in the center of Father's atrium. Her maids were about her, pouring in fragrant oils and washing her back; others were airing out the silk bedcovers and pillows — it is no coincidence that her name means "pleasure seeker." I recognized the high voice of her favorite male slave, singing from behind a lattice partition. He was playing a lyre, the small harp preferred in our royal court.

"What is it, little Cleopatra?" Tryphaena asked me, lifting her eyebrows with boredom.

"Where is Father?" I asked her. "When is he coming

back?" To show her I was not leaving until she answered, I removed my sandals. A maid took them and handed me a linen towel. I folded it and placed it on one of the benches so I could sit without feeling the cold marble against my legs.

At this, my sister raised herself out of the pool. "You <u>dare</u> to sit in my presence?" she said. Two guards, who were standing on the balcony, took one step toward me, touching the swords that were strapped to their waists.

I am careful what I say to this sister. She is ten years older than I, and because I am just twelve, she rules over me by that fact alone. I lowered my eyes to show respect.

"When you are queen, Tryphaena, I will kneel before you."

She sunk back into the pool up to her shoulders then raised her hand, snapping her fingers. A Nubian girl wearing a brown tunic appeared with a tray. A goblet of wine and a bowl of figs were offered to me.

I could feel my insides shaking. Would this sister try to poison me? Yes, I believe so. As for my other older sister, Berenice — never! She and I adore each other even though I am eight years younger.

I took the wine and raised it toward Tryphaena as if

toasting her, but really I was watching the liquid, looking for an oil perhaps floating on its surface, or powder sticking to the sides of the cup. If I suspected poison and tossed the wine into the pool, she would have her guards behead me on the spot. If it was indeed poison, one sip and I could die.

I raised the cup to my lips and tasted no bitterness on the rim. My eyes closed as I took the first sip, as if savoring such an excellent taste, but really my thought was, *O Isis, I am afraid.* But does Isis hear a girl's prayer? My heart raced as I drank, my stomach turned with nervousness, or was it from a fearsome death beginning in me?

Three sips later, I returned the goblet to the tray, then reached for a fig which I rolled between my fingers. It felt sticky. Tryphaena looked at me through narrowed eyes as a cat might look at a tiny bird, trying to decide if a capture is worth the effort. After a moment, she tipped her head back to soak her hair in the water. When her eyes closed, I returned the fig to the bowl and wiped my hand on my chiton.

A maid leaned over the pool with a tiny jar of oil, which she poured over Tryphaena's scalp then combed through her dark hair. I waited for my sister to speak, counting my heartbeats, a wonderful relief flooding over me that I was alive.

"Now then, Cleopatra," she said, her eyes still closed for the dripping water, "what was it you wanted to know about our father?"

I stood and took my sandals from the maid. "May our father be blessed that you occupy his rooms," I said.

Evening

Now it is twilight. The wind has quieted and I can see that the waves have also. The ocean is becoming a darker blue as night nears. O, where is Father? I hope he can see the lighthouse on Pharos Island. I know its bright light is meant for sailors approaching our harbor, but I think it is also for kings who sleep in a lonely place.

I am ready to put away this paper and cheer myself with a bath. First, I must check the underground fire room to make sure the slaves have not fallen asleep again. This is something that enrages Tryphaena. She demands they keep the coals going at all times, fanning hot air through pipes under the floors (so she can soak at any hour of the day or night).

Thinking of Tryphaena makes me tired. I hope she is elsewhere in the palace tonight, perhaps reclining on her couch in the banquet hall. *O Isis, let the wine put her to sleep quickly!*

Arrow, my sweet old leopard, has jumped onto my bed, purring loudly. Her front paws are as big as my hands, and she is now licking those paws to wash her long, silvery whiskers. Moments ago, she finished eating a thick chunk of roasted lamb given to her by the royal cook.

"Good cat," I tell her, stroking her huge spotted head, as I have every night since she was a kitten. Once I fall asleep, Arrow will leave my chamber to roam the dark gardens. Since she has just been fed, she will not bother our little cats who are out hunting mice and beetles.

But woe to intruders: A leopard hides in the shadows of our palace walls.

7 Januarius

This morning, early, I slipped out to the tomb of King Alexander the Great, the founder of our city. It is near enough to the palace so that I was back before my sisters were awake.

The building is marble with open sides and steps leading down to the tomb, candles on every ledge. Because guards are here day and night, it is safe for me to come by myself.

I knelt at the side of his coffin. A glass dome covers it, but the glass is an older type, pitted with sand in places and rippled, as if one were looking through dark water. When Alexander died of a fever in Babylon, his body was brought back to Egypt and embalmed in the same manner as our pharaohs. The embalmers painted his cheeks and lips red. His hair is a golden yellow with an orange tint above his forehead. If this is paint, I do not know. Though he is a mummy, he still appears to be about thirty years old.

Alexander lies on his back, his hands folded across his chest, wearing an embroidered Persian vest buttoned at his waist. A skirt made of thin leather strips comes down to his knees. Draped over his shoulder is a beautiful scarlet cloak, the wool still untouched by moths. I wish I could see what type of sandals he is wearing, but a shield of hammered gold covers his feet.

Did I mention that Alexander the Great has been dead for nearly three hundred years?

Father says there are ancient Hebrew prophecies about a king, a messiah, who will bring peace and forgiveness. This king will have lived for a time in Egypt. When he dies, his body will not decay. He will rise from the dead, and all other kings will bow down to him. All nations will serve him; the government will be on his shoulders.

Some people in this city believe that because Alexander already conquered so much of the world and was in Egypt, he might be the messiah, thus the many guards to protect his tomb.

I keep coming to look at Alexander, to see if he shows life. Not yet. (If the glass breaks, will he start to rot?)

THE NEXT AFTERNOON

Caravans arrived today from Gilead and Arabia. Their camels were loaded with treasures that will be traded for our grain. The merchants have pitched their striped tents outside the city wall near the canal that brings Nile water to Lake Mareotis. I watched from my roof garden, glad the stench of camels cannot reach me, though I always enjoy hearing the bells and bangles that hang from their saddles.

When I saw some of our slaves carrying chests toward the palace, I was too excited to wait on the roof. I ran down the inside steps to wait in the courtyard. Berenice and Tryphaena were already there, of course.

As princesses, we are the first in Alexandria to run our fingers through the sacks of spices, pinching small amounts to flick in the air like perfume. The courtyard was soon filled with the sweet aromas of cinnamon, myrrh, cassia, and frankincense. My sisters and I also are the first to unwrap the parcels of silk. This fabric is so delicate we can see through it, and when we throw a piece in the air it floats down slowly. When we were younger, we used to run with it back and forth through the halls and around the columns, in and out, the silk flying from our outstretched hands like lovely colored flags.

But now that Tryphaena is so much older, she sits on a stool while bowing servants bring everything to her. To-day, she unfolded the silks as if they were dirty bed linens, then tossed them aside, bored. Next, she pushed a chest with her foot until it tipped over. Out spilled an elegant array of bracelets and sashes, Persian slippers, mirrors, and ivory hair ornaments. Berenice and I glanced at each other. These things were much too beautiful to be thrown on the floor.

Then Tryphaena reached into a wooden crate and dug through the straw to uncover hundreds of tiny alabaster jars. She uncorked one. Instantly there was the wonderful scent of almond oil. (How I love to rub it into my skin after a bath.) She sniffed it, frowned, then opened other jars. There was coconut oil, fine perfumes, and the balm of Gilead itself, a most prized item.

The last chest to be opened was full of jewels and necklaces. I saw a rope of pearls that was so exquisite I could not help myself. As I started to clasp it around my neck, Tryphaena grabbed a dagger from inside her dress and placed it against my throat. I felt the sharp edge scrape my skin.

Slowly, I handed the pearls to my sister and backed out of the room.

8 Januarius, just before sunset

Five days have passed since Father disappeared. The snake that killed his slave Mento is still loose in the palace. Its moist trail was seen last night near the bath. Servants are looking everywhere, but it hides itself well. I am careful where I step and where I sit.

This morning, Arrow and I were in one of the small

palace courtyards, enjoying the winter sunlight, when I heard shouts. I could see Tryphaena down a hallway, pacing back and forth, her arms waving angrily. She was yelling at an official who held a scroll and who seemed to be pleading with her.

I overheard words that brought joy to my heart. Father is alive! He is still king and he has sent a message to my sister:

If she doesn't stop pretending to be queen, he will have her executed.

At this, I slipped away so she would not see me, Arrow quietly at my side.

TO CONTINUE . . .

For the rest of the morning, I wandered along the harbor with Neva, my favorite maid. We were dressed in the linen chitons of common Greek girls so we could pass unnoticed among the fishermen. Rather than have her carry my sandals as usual, I held them myself so we would appear as two equals. I <u>can</u> look plain and unroyal when I want to. Also, because I am able to speak with native Egyptians in their own language, I can mingle in the agora, the marketplace, without drawing attention to myself — a privacy I much enjoy. If commoners know a princess walks among them, they will either smother her with affection or bother her about problems that belong to the king.

One of my favorite guards, Puzo, followed at a discreet distance. He is from the island of Sicily, but as a youth he was enslaved by the Romans and trained as a gladiator. He was fierce and proud, often compared to the famous Spartacus. When he was sent to Alexandria for the amusement of my father, I bought his freedom before he was forced to fight. Ever since, Puzo has kept me safe. When we are in public together, if I wish not to be noticed, he disguises himself, often as an Arab in a *dishdasha*, a flowing white robe.

Near the water's edge, Neva and I met a Hebrew man selling figs and barley loaves from his cart. We purchased enough for our midday meal, then walked out to Pharos Island on the Heptastadion. This is the stone bridge that is high enough for boats to sail under, from our east harbor to the west. It is one mile long. Out here we can speak privately. Small tide pools among the rocks draw flocks of seagulls that shriek and cry with a noise loud enough to keep anyone nearby from hearing our conversation.

Neva is pure Macedonian Greek, like I am, descended from the royal servants of Ptolemy I. I, of course, am descended from Ptolemy himself. Though Neva and I share the same light skin and blue eyes and could pass as sisters, we are content with our inherited roles: she as maid, I as princess. A skilled listener makes a good friend, and this perfectly describes Neva. She is a few years older than I, perhaps she is fifteen. I trust her with my life; my secrets are hers — to my knowledge she has never betrayed a confidence. This morning as we stepped around the tide pools, there were two things I wanted to tell her.

I fear Father will be murdered. And if he is, I, Cleopatra, want to be, and should be, queen.

This may seem an odd confession, but my thoughts are sound. Father has six living children by his two wives long dead. I have no memory of my mother for I was quite small when she died.

Father's daughters are Tryphaena, Berenice, myself, and little Arsinoë. His sons are just babies, Ptolemy One and Ptolemy the Younger. Of all my siblings I am the only one who can speak the language of native Egyptians and other foreigners who live in our beautiful Alexandria.

For reasons unknown to myself, the gods have gifted me with learning tongues. Just from my daily visits to the agora and fishing villages, I have learned to speak with the peasants from Ethiopia, Syria, and Arabia. I am beginning to better understand the Hebrew scholars by studying in the Library and Mouseion, our great learning center dedicated to the nine Muses. The Muses, of course, are our goddesses of poetry, music, art, and so forth.

This gift of befriending people will make me a better queen than Tryphaena, who hates the Jews and the Medes. It will help me be better than Berenice, the sister I love, who is too afraid of the streets to venture out of our royal apartments. A queen <u>must</u> understand her subjects and care for them. This describes me! I am sorry to say this about Arsinoë because she is just nine years old, but she is as spoiled and mean as our eldest sister, Tryphaena.

If Father is killed, then one of us will become pharaoh. O, I do not want him to die, but I do want to be ready if necessary to be Egypt's ruler, the best ever known. I must apply myself to gain wisdom.

To continue . . .

After eating our meal, Neva and I walked in the wet sand below the lighthouse, where the tiniest waves roll in. Puzo sat on the jetty looking like an Arab in deep thought, but I knew he was watching me with a protective eye.

Because this beach is protected from wind and surf, it is warm even in winter. We waded up to our knees, swishing our hands in the cold water and splashing our faces. It was so refreshing I did it again and again, happy that I had not allowed Neva to paint me with cosmetics this morning. The black ocher stings my eyes if not washed off carefully.

The nearer I am to the ocean, the more content I feel. I love smelling the salt air and watching the waves break against the outer rocks. Far out to sea the horizon looks bumpy with specks of white. This time of year, the Mediterranean is empty of ships because the wind is too wild. Though Rome is a long ocean voyage to the northwest, Father has worried for years about pirates or, worse, a surprise attack from Julius Caesar.

Curses on him, the barbarian! His cruel legions march wherever they are ordered, conquering lands with their catapults and siege machines. Father has told me we will not let him have Egypt, ever, especially our beloved city, Alexandria.

We are a sovereign state. The Roman Empire shall not conquer us.

That is why our royal fleet keeps ready for battle by having its sailors mend sails and lines, and the soldiers practice their weapons. The oarsmen, who are our strongest slaves from Ethiopia, keep alert by rowing the warships out into the rough waves, then back again, day after day no matter the weather.

It is dark now. Moments ago I walked out on my terrace to watch the remains of the sun on the sea. In our eastern harbor, torches were being lit on our little island called Antirrhodus. Here among the rocks sits a beautiful little palace that I secretly call my own, but it really belongs to the entire royal family.

Inside the island palace are several golden statues of my father, the king, posing like a sphinx, also there are marble busts of my older sisters and myself. The artist who carved my likeness sculpted me with an Egyptian headdress and a cobra, but truly I prefer wearing my hair in the Greek style, without such heavy adornments.

12 JANUARIUS

It is evening again. I will sleep well now, knowing Father is safe from the crowds who threaten him. He is hiding somewhere up the Nile, his exact whereabouts known only by his closest advisers.

I have sent Puzo with another guard to observe Tryphaena in case she is up to evil. Neva has readied my cushions and lit a small lamp with cinnamon oil, and is now resting on her pallet at the foot of my bed. She will not let herself sleep until I do. I look at Neva's sweet face and thank the gods for her loyalty.

Did I mention that she is my reader, as well? During my bath is when I most love to hear her voice. Today, I listened for an hour as she read from Homer's *Odyssey*, one of my favorite poems. She does it so dramatically, too. We both love this adventure of Odysseus that describes his voyage home after the battle of Troy.

Out the window the sea looks black except for a flicker of light flashing across the waves. This is the beacon from our lighthouse that burns all day and all night, a comfort for those of us living on this northern point of Africa. The only thing I do not like about this perpetual flame is that if the Romans are marching this way or are foolish enough to sail through winter storms, they will easily find us.

There is no hiding in darkness if there is even one spark of light.

To continue . . .

Just a few moments ago, Berenice came in to show me her hair. Her maid had braided it into dozens of tiny rows, in the style of native Nubians.

"Look, Cleopatra," she said, turning on her feet as a dancer does. Lamplight reflected off the assorted gems that had been woven into her braids, some were rubies, others were diamonds. I suspect these had been stolen from Father's jewelry chest for I had never seen her with so many.

Berenice wore two silk chitons, one draped over the other to show layers of blue and emerald, an elegant look. She wore gold bracelets on each bare arm. Her eyes were shadowed with violet and black liner, her earrings were pearl.

"You look beautiful," I said, knowing that was what she

wanted to hear and because she is, indeed, beautiful. What I shall not tell her is how foolish she looks with tiny gold rings in her left nostril, three of them! It looks slavish and common.

Then she glided out of my chamber and disappeared down the hall. Another banquet with dancers and musicians await her, no doubt Tryphaena is already there.

Tonight I am happy to be just twelve years old, too young to be expected at royal parties.

My only worry at this moment is the puff adder still sliding along the floors somewhere in the palace. We keep finding its curved track in hallways, courtyards, and in our private chambers. This horrifies me! Whoever set it on my father's bed many days ago is probably happily waiting to hear of the next victim. I have told Arrow to catch the snake, but who can tell a cat what to do? I gathered my fingers in the fur around her neck and looked sternly in her golden eyes as I gave her my order. She blinked. Once, twice, then she batted my shoulder with her huge paw before turning away to do what she pleases. Arrow is too spoiled to care about a snake.

The fragrance of Berenice's perfume lingers pleasantly as I ready myself for bed. My hourglass has run out. *O Isis, please let me sleep safely tonight.*

The next morning

Early, just at sunrise, Berenice and I visited the docks. We watched the royal zookeepers carry a cage down the ramp with a new lioness and her two mewing cubs inside. They were captured last month far up the Nile, and brought to Alexandria. Word is that Julius Caesar himself has requested them to battle his gladiators. (I am pleased that Puzo is spared forever from this horrible amusement.) Also on the barge was a baby baboon, an orphan apparently. Berenice thought it looked so sweet swinging from its cage that she has taken it from the zoo back to the palace.

I do love this sister, but she is not very imaginative. What did she name her little pet? "Baboon." That is it. Berenice might be beautiful, but she would not make an interesting queen.

In the early evening, I went to the royal stables. Bucephalus, my beautiful white Arabian, stomped in her stall when she saw me. I have not ridden her in two weeks and I miss her. I named her after King Alexander's war horse, which carried him into battle as far as India. When Bucephalus died, Alexander built a magnificent city to surround the tomb.

I wrapped my arms around her big neck. She snorted. Then she tossed her head, her white mane stinging my face, a playful habit ever since she was a filly. She nudged my arm until I brought out the treat hiding in my belt — a small square of honeycomb.

"Here, Bucephalus," I said. "Good girl."

Her brown eye watched me as I stroked her neck. A thick ivory comb hung on the gate next to my saddle. When I reached for it, she butted my hand, knocking it down to the straw. She dislikes having her mane untangled, so today I just returned the comb to its hook.

You wild thing, I thought in my heart. *You lovely wild thing.* O, I envy her freedom, that she is without cares or worries.

This evening as I was bathing and listening to Neva read, my younger sister, Arsinoë, marched into my chamber. Her dress was blue with a purple sash, and she was barefoot except for ornaments jingling on her ankles. She was followed by her nurse and three of her little barking dogs. I call them The Toads for their noses look squashed and wet.

She tugged at her nurse's skirt because she was too excited to speak for herself. Her nurse bowed.

"Your Highness," she said to me, "Arsinoë wants you to find a new playmate for her. She is tired of her brothers and wants a Pygmy child to amuse her."

Sinking low into my bath, I splashed warm water on my face for time to think. Arisinoë's last request was for a child from the Dinka tribe. They are a graceful, gentle people who can grow to be more than seven feet tall. A Dinka girl was captured near her home up the Nile and brought to the palace, but she died from a fever after a few days.

Father has given me the authority to grant any requests of my younger siblings. I enjoy this responsibility for in my heart I am practicing to be queen. But as for a Pygmy child? I do not intend to give my sister everything she asks for.

"I will see what I can do, Arsinoë. Now go to bed."

15 JANUARIUS

I spent the morning at the Library and Mouseion, where new toys and machines are often invented. As these buildings are connected to the palace, I am free to be myself — to speak in Greek and to wear my dress with the royal purple veil, Arrow at my side. She stands as tall as my waist so I rest my hand on her back as we wander about.

As usual, Neva came with me. Unlike the times when we walk side by side along the beach or in the agora, she remained three steps behind me to show respect. Puzo stood in a doorway, his arms crossed. Today he wore a short Egyptian skirt made of leather.

In the Library, we came upon my friend Olympus, studying on a bench beneath a window. Sunshine pours into the halls and atria here, giving good light for reading. Though he's fourteen years to my twelve, he is already studying to be a physician and hopes one day to work for the royal family. His father is originally from Athens and is one of the philosophers we have appointed. These learned men have amazing ideas, as do our astronomers and scientists. But Father wants these ideas to stay within the palace walls, for if peasants hear too many new things, they might revolt. We need them to work our fields and fish the rivers, not to sit and think. Father says that this is the only way for the House of Ptolemy to stay in power, that thinking is for the noble class. I am not sure if this is right, but it is true.

Olympus smiled when he saw me. His short chiton

was tied at the waist, and he wore a leather pouch that holds his writing tools. A secret he and I share is that we write notes to each other! This seems curious because we see each other often, but it has proven to be an easy way to "talk" without people spying on us. His letters are so clever I have saved them. They are locked securely in the little chest by my bed.

I remained standing while Olympus rolled up the papyrus he had been reading. He climbed onto a stool to slide the scroll into a hole in the wall where dozens and dozens are stored. The wall looks like a giant honeycomb. In fact, there are many of these throughout the Library, filling entire rooms up to the ceiling. The knob on each scroll has a string attached to it with a little tag that hangs out over the shelf. This way the next reader will be able to identify its contents, for we have the ancient writings of Aristotle and Plato as well as the Hebrew prophets. When a breeze moves through the halls, these tags flutter like hundreds of tiny white butterflies. (Homer's poem about Odysseus is also here. I have read it twice.)

Stepping down from the stool, he leaned close enough to whisper, "I have bad news, Cleopatra."

I did not answer. For a moment I just wanted to look at

his face. His eyes are gentle, and his hair curls onto his forehead in the Greek style. His beard will be blond when it grows out, but for now there is just a light fuzz on his cheeks and chin.

He took my arm with the familiarity of a childhood playmate, not concerned with my royal status. He led me to a courtyard where there was a fountain. Neva and Puzo stood at a distance, but I wish they had been next to me when Olympus gave his terrible report.

"A plot has been discovered," he said. "The hearts of the people are filled with schemes to do wrong — they want your father dead. Assassins are searching for him as we speak."

To continue . . .

I lowered myself onto a seat by the pool. Cool blue mosaics cover the shallow bottom; the fountain pours over the side into a smaller pool. Arrow settled herself at my feet, her two front paws stretched out in front of her. I sat quietly stroking her head as Olympus continued. He spoke in a low voice so the noise of water would muffle his words should anyone try to hear us.

He explained a dark truth: As Pharaoh, Father is hated by nearly everyone in Egypt, especially the villagers who live along the Nile. Not only has he mismanaged the government's money and taxed everyone unfairly, Father ordered that any new silver coin being minted must have two-thirds of the silver left out!

This means that in the agora or on the docks, a man's money is now worth only one-third of what it used to be. I do not blame people for being angry.

But how can I, Princess of the Nile, help them? And how can I keep them from murder? I remained calm while Olympus talked. Calm, that is, until he described Father's plan.

He wants the Romans to come to Alexandria with all their troops! He wants them to punish our angry villagers so he can come out of hiding and reclaim his throne. Father has already promised to pay ten thousand talents to a wealthy Roman money lender if he will hire these soldiers.

At this news my heart despaired, and even though bright sunshine filled the courtyard, I began to shiver. I struggled for composure, as a princess must, but felt anxious. Egypt could be doomed if Father follows through with his plans. He knows as well as the rest of us that if the Romans land here and stake down their tents, they will never leave us alone. These soldiers are the strongest, most fearless men in the world.

Has Father lost his mind? *Maybe he is just drunk again, I thought, for he does worship Dionysus, the god of wine.*

"When does my father, the king, plan to leave?" I asked Olympus, shading my eyes with my hand to look at him. Anyone spying on us might think we were merely discussing the weather.

"Early spring," he answered. "Before the vernal equinox."

I calculated. Winter should be ending in several weeks. Then ships would resume traveling the open seas. If one counts by the moons, there are just eight months a year that ocean voyages can be safe from storms and foul winds. Father could sail to Rome and back by autumn.

I wish in my heart that he would just send a letter asking Julius Caesar for help, instead of making such a long journey. But letters have been known to get lost or stolen, and Father says there is nothing like eye-to-eye contact to get a man to agree with you. I hope he is right.

O Isis, I am frightened. If Father does go to Caesar to ask for help, who will be here to protect me from Tryphaena? She will take the throne in his absence, I know it, and put watchful, hateful eyes on me.

While I adore Berenice, she _is_ second in line to be queen. What worries me is that her softness causes her to be easily influenced. Will she be loyal to Father, or will she share in the schemes of Tryphaena? As for my little sister and brothers, they still sleep in the nursery and play with toys. Although Arsinoë is old enough to want a Pygmy playmate, she is no threat to me.

Evening

There was quite an upset at our meal tonight. Berenice brought her new pet along, to recline with her on the couch. But when Baboon saw the food, he refused to sit still. He leaped onto the table where plates of oysters were beautifully displayed with cucumbers and sea urchins (my _favorite_ dish). Baboon helped himself.

Before we could rescue the meal, Baboon found the bowl of onions and scooped them out with his tiny hands. They fell from the table and rolled along the floor like white marbles. Meanwhile, Tryphaena stood up, furious.

She clapped her hands and ordered some servants to catch "the wretched creature." But dinner was ruined. Three men throwing themselves at a squirming animal made a mess of our table.

I am eating tonight in my room. Neva just brought in a nice soup, leek, I believe, with a fresh cooked duck egg and bread for dipping.

16 JANUARIUS, MORNING

I am writing this early; the sun will rise in moments.

After last night's sleep, I feel rested. Now that I have had time to think, some hope is unfolding inside me.

Not long ago, perhaps two years past, Father "bought" a friendship with Rome. He borrowed six thousand talents of silver from our government to pay Julius Caesar and Pompey so that Rome and Egypt would be allies. Pompey, a vigorous soldier, is also called the Bearded Executioner. In just three months, he rid the Mediterranean of pirates — 846 ships — who had been plundering vessels on the trade routes. This fearless Pompey also captured Jerusalem a few years ago, leaving Roman soldiers in charge.

He is not a man I would want for an enemy. Thus when

I suddenly remembered that Pompey is my patron, that he was paid to protect us royal children, I felt enormous relief.

Since we are "friends," maybe the soldiers will be satisfied with just camping on our shores until the trouble calms down.

Father now owes sixteen thousand talents. If it takes years for an Egyptian laborer to earn just one talent, it would take many laborers many years to pay Father's debt. What does a poor man gain from his toil?

Now I understand why common, hardworking people hate my father so deeply. My heart despairs over this.

As I write this, Arrow has curled herself at my chair with one heavy paw resting on my foot. Her long, spotted tail is tucked under her chin like a cushion. What a good, old friend! Tomorrow I am going to ask the royal jeweler to make a new collar for her, a beautiful one, perhaps gold with royal purple stones.

The sand in my hourglass is almost at the bottom, my oil lamp is low. To bed now . . .

17 Januarius

I have turned my thoughts to what Olympus said the other day, and I believe him for he is wise beyond his years. He studies with learned men at the Mouseion and he is also friends with commoners such as cooks and chariot drivers. He listens to what people say. This is a quality that will make him a good physician, but in the meantime it makes him my valuable friend.

Since I wanted to see and hear for myself what our subjects are saying about Father, I planned a visit to the agora. With Neva's help, I washed all color from my face and replaced my gold necklace with a seashell pendant. She combed my hair into the style of Greek girls, and we dressed in simple chitons, no perfume or earrings. We wore thin wool shawls as a northern wind had returned, making the day cold.

Early in the morning, we hurried on our errands to buy bread and little cakes, Puzo melting into the crowds behind us. This outing was just an excuse because, truth is, I have plenty of bread — the royal bakers deliver fresh loaves to me twice daily.

As usual, the streets were crowded with pushing,

shoving, and shouting people — a babble of languages. Some odors were so unpleasant I drew a veil over my nose and mouth. This is one reason Berenice will not appear in public. She does not understand foreigners, particularly those who do not bathe as often as we Greeks do. Her delicate stomach makes her afraid of new foods, though she is more likely to die of poisoning within her own walls! Myself, I do love the smell of roasting meat and I love the clamor of crowds.

Thus Neva and I slowly made our way through the streets. We were pressed in on all sides and many times I was pinched by unseen hands . . . rudely pinched! But such is the risk of pretending to be a common girl and not allowing Puzo to stay by my side. If I brought my official guards, then everyone would know I am from the palace. With murderers looking for Father, all the more I needed to conceal my identity.

I turned down an alley that was so narrow my shoulders brushed the walls as I sidestepped puddles and piles of dung. Neva followed me, her hand hooked in my sash so we would not lose each other. We passed a doorway where a man sat on his heels. Behind him was his little store. The back wall was dark except for a small oil lamp that illuminated shelves of idols for sale, all sizes, carved from stone and wood. The length of the alley was dotted with stalls like this, their owners crouched in doorways, leering at us as we hurried past, reaching out a dirty hand.

We ran into a bright busy street and once again blended into the crowd. I could see an Arab in his flowing *dishdasha*, a braided cord around his forehead, watching me. Dear Puzo. Once again I felt safe. When I noticed people swarming around something, I bent down to look between all the elbows and arms and saw a square cage, full of baby crocodiles, each about the length of my arm. They were writhing and snapping their jaws. I doubt they had been fed in many days. Children were poking sticks and reeds into the cage, apparently not realizing their fingers could be bitten off.

The owner of the crocodiles was a tiny black man, a Pygmy, who stood on top of the cage shouting terrible curses on my father, shouting that his crocodiles were for sale, cheap, to anyone willing to sneak them into the king's bed. The crowd roared with pleasure, by no means understanding that such an act would get them beheaded.

My heart was so troubled at this, I pulled Neva's arm and we hurried away, down toward the wharves. Near the eastern harbor there is a spit of land with rocks that form a breakwater. Nearby is the Temple of Isis, our Egyptian goddess.

We climbed the steps and entered the place of worship. It is a large, open room with a wide view of the sea. Always there is a breeze. In the heat of the summer this breeze is refreshing, but now during winter it is just cold.

I lay a small ball of incense that I had carried in my pouch at the stone feet of Isis. An attendant stepped from the shadows carrying a lantern which he used to light my offering. The steps surrounding Isis were lined with candles floating in bowls of oil. They flickered as a slave lifted a fan of ostrich feathers and began waving it over me.

O Isis, I prayed, *protect my father. Protect me. I sense there is more danger than I can see.*

To continue . . .

Neva and I left the temple to walk along the cold beach, Puzo far behind. A crowd had gathered in the sand. Entertaining them was a Psylloi, one of the many African snake charmers who roam the streets of Alexandria. I watched the cobra rise out of its basket, its hood flared as it swayed. People were tossing coins into a dish and applauding, pleased by the snake's dance. Do they not know that cobras are deaf to flute music? They only flare because they are angry and ready to spit their killing poison. I have witnessed men being struck dead while showing off.

Nearby, two boys standing knee-deep in the waves were pulling in a fishing net. They started to sing. It was a wicked song that made my blood chill, wicked because it was about King Ptolemy and his daughter Cleopatra — me! I felt myself begin to tremble as the song grew louder. Part of it went like this:

> . . . *a poisoned cup*
> *a serpent's bite*
> *a sword to the neck*
> *would be just right.*

Wanting to hear no more I pushed my way through the crowd, back along the Canopic Way to the palace, Neva following. We slipped in by one of the servants' gates. Before changing out of my clothes, I took a tablet and rubbed the wax until it was smooth enough to write upon. When finished, I lay a blank tablet face-to-face, and tied them together with string, then lit a purple candle. Dripping the wax on to the string, I pressed my ring into the wax for a personal seal.

"Take this to Olympus," I instructed Neva.

He had been right. Father's life was in danger. And so was mine.

19 Januarius

Arrow is wearing her new collar. When she paces through the halls at night, I can see torchlight reflecting off the tiny amethysts, my favorite purple stone. They are set in gold with black etchings: Hieroglyphs spell her name and mine.

Olympus and I have been sending tablets to each other twice a day. I have written him that the songs in the streets have put fear in my heart, so this morning we met in the Gymnasion to watch the wrestlers and to talk about these things. We sat in the stands near the athletes where their chatter could drown out our voices. O, his friendship is a comfort.

I have been reflecting on something that gladdens my

heart. With Olympus sitting next to me I forget that I am royal and he is common. Maybe it is the bold way he speaks his mind, often leaning over to touch my arm until I nod with understanding. Then when I am the one speaking, he listens carefully to every word, looking at me with such tenderness I end up pouring out my heart to him. Olympus will be a great physician, I know it. Though he is young like myself, I trust him deeply.

But he is worried about my safety. He has heard ugly rumors about me, and this morning he saw something disturbing at the stables.

The riding master showed Olympus a square piece of papyrus that had been nailed to Bucephalus' stall. On it was painted drawings showing the Ptolemy children: the three youngest were sleeping peacefully in cradles, the two eldest — Tryphaena and Berenice — were gazing at their reflections in a mirror, but the third daughter — me — was missing her head!

When Olympus brought this papyrus to me, my heart fell. I do not know exactly what it means or who wants to kill me. It is common knowledge that I am Father's favorite daughter, so perhaps the people who hate him, hate me as well, because I am the one he most likely would name to succeed him.

In any event, it is now too dangerous for me to ride Bucephalus, even out in the desert. Enemies know my favorite oasis, where we always rest before returning to the city. My heart is uneasy knowing that I am being watched.

Thus, Olympus has started making plans, but what they are, he will not say. Not until everything is in place.

22 JANUARIUS

Last night before the moon rose, Neva and I made our way down the palace steps that lead to the water's edge. Puzo waited with a small boat. In the darkness he rowed us out to my island, Antirrhodus. I wanted to be alone, that is, without all the servants and guards who are usually at my call.

As we neared the island's beach, Puzo jumped into the water to pull the boat ashore. I lifted my chiton so it would not get wet and stepped over the rail to the sand. The usual torches lit the entryway to my little palace, but I wanted to walk for a while along the dark shoreline. After some moments, Puzo ran to me and hurried us back to the boat. He carried something white and round under his arm.

I did not understand why we had to leave Antirrhodus so quickly, but I trusted Puzo. When he launched us back into the waves and started rowing, the object he had set on the floor at his feet rolled toward me.

It was a human skull. Even in the dim light I could see my name painted across the forehead.

I am sick at heart . . . another message that someone wants me dead. But who?

Princess Cleopatra to Olympus, loyal friend and observer:

Mercy to you and peace. Your last letter so frightened me, I rubbed out the words so that you will not be suspected.

Yes, I will be ready. Do not tell a soul, not even little Arsinoë or my brothers. Their nurses can make up a story if they wonder where I have gone. By the time Tryphaena and Berenice figure it out, I will be safe.

I will leave Arrow in your care, my friend. Please see that she is well fed, otherwise she gets extremely rough. If Cook runs out of lamb, there are plenty of rats in the grainery, plump and sweet to her taste. She enjoys an ostrich egg from time to *time. Also, Bucephalus will need exercise and your tender touch. <u>Do not</u> try to comb her mane.*

Thank you in advance, dear Olympus. I know we will be seeing each other between now and my departure, but might not be able to speak aloud of our plans, thus these instructions for my beloved pets.

I am happy that Neva will be my companion on this journey, but my heart would take delight if you, too, could be at my side, Olympus.

16 FEBRUARIUS

I wait. Olympus will send word when it is time.

My guards stay near, even when I bathe, though they stand behind a screen with the harpist. In addition to a sword, Puzo also has small daggers strapped to the inside of each sandal; his gold armbands are woven with chains that can quickly be thrown around an enemy's neck to strangle him. Death takes just a few seconds. I've watched him practice this on prisoners who were to be executed. Not a pleasant sight.

Though I know Puzo is always ready to defend my life

with his, I still am not sleeping well and my stomach is nervous. In my heart I fear being poisoned, so I have assigned a new slave to taste my food. I do not know his name, I do not <u>want</u> to know his name, but he is still alive, thank the gods.

Because my life is in danger, Neva and I have not explored the agora in four weeks, nor visited the stables. Poor Bucephalus is left to the care of the horse master. Yesterday, another note was nailed to her stall, with a warning: If I am seen petting her, an assassin will be waiting to throw a spear through both of us. O, this causes me anguish. Who is it that wants me dead and where are they? Can they see me now?

I spend many hours listening to Neva read, but when her voice grows weary I walk to the Library to meet Olympus. As he is fluent in Latin as well as his native Greek, he has been helping me learn to speak as the Romans do. It is a harsh language that sounds like pigs grunting in my opinion, but I am determined to communicate with the barbarians if need be. I will be wiser if I understand their precise words. Did I mention that one of his favorite exercises is to translate Latin into Greek and Greek into Latin? He said this helps him develop his vocabulary and writing skills.

Olympus and I also enjoy spending time with our good friend Theophilus, who lives in the eastern part of the city in the Jewish Quarter. His ancestor was one of the seventy men who translated Hebrew Scriptures into Greek, and this translation of the Torah is called the Septuagint. For reasons unknown to me, there are as many Jews living here in Alexandria as in Jerusalem; their synagogue is huge. The three of us have spent hours in the courtyard, talking together and discussing our different religions. O, I enjoy their companionship! They told me I am wasting my time visiting Alexander the Great. He is not the messiah, his body will stay in that tomb until someone buries it or dumps it in the sea. They feel quite strongly about this.

Theophilus, whose name means "One Who Loves God," says his family is descended from Moses, the Jew who led their people out of Egypt. I have reflected on this and asked him why the Jews came back to Egypt if they had wanted so badly to leave. Our conversation was interrupted by a messenger who bowed quickly, then reported to me that King Ptolemy's ship was heading out to sea for Rome.

I jumped up. *No,* I thought, *it cannot be.*

In minutes I had returned to the palace, disguised

myself, and was hurrying with Neva through the streets. We ran the long mile over the Heptastodion to Pharos Island, Puzo this time dressed as a poor fisherman. From the top of the lighthouse I would be able to see for myself if Father had returned from hiding and was now leaving Alexandria.

The lighthouse master is an old, bent man. He knows I am a princess in disguise, but he will never betray me. Years ago when he lived in Rome, he was caught gossiping about Julius Caesar and was given a choice: to be executed, crucified on a cross like a common Roman criminal, or to have his tongue cut out. He chose life. But without his tongue, he will never again be able to speak.

I asked him what ship had left the harbor. Was it Father's?

"No," he gestured, "come see for yourself."

He led us inside. The ground floor is shaped like a huge square, with offices and storage and sleeping rooms. Stacks of firewood fill two sides. There are many types of wood, some brought down the Nile from our jungles, some from the forests of Phoenicia.

I looked straight up. Two spiral ramps with steps cut into them twist upward, far up to the top, where the lantern sits like the flame on a giant candle. A donkey was pulling a cart loaded with wood up one of these ramps, and another was coming down the other ramp.

All day, all night, the great fire must be fed.

To continue . . .

The lighthouse master motioned us to follow him, but to keep as close to the wall as possible. There are no railings. One missed step and we would fall to our deaths. I worried this could happen because the ramp was slippery from donkey dung, and a bitter stench made me feel sick. With one hand I held a veil over my nose; the other hand I firmly pressed against the stone wall. As we passed each small open window, the breeze refreshed me. I could see blue ocean far, far below us.

The sight was dizzying. For a moment I imagined myself falling, a thought so vivid my heart raced. But, O, the view!

The sea blended so perfectly with the sky I couldn't tell where one began and the other ended. Below us the city looked like tiny building blocks had been arranged by a child, white marble blocks gleaming in the sun. The streets were dark strips between the blocks, moving slowly like a stream of ants. Beyond the palace I recognized the Hippodrome. Dotting its track were miniature chariots pulled by miniature horses, circling around and around. They looked like my brothers' toys! Nearby were the stables, though I could not catch sight of my Bucephalus.

Far to the west were the vast yellow sands of the Sahara with a green mark near the coast, an oasis perhaps? And in the other direction, the Nile flowed into the Mediterranean. Now I know what birds see, I thought. Are the gods up here, too, looking down on us as if we were ants? Can Isis see me? Is she up here or is she in her temple?

The higher we climbed the more the walls slanted in. The air was hot from a loud, roaring furnace directly overhead, the mighty beacon of Alexandria. My neck ached from looking up. I could see a high ledge outside one of the windows where a statue of Poseidon looks out over the ocean.

A man wearing an iron mask and iron netting over his shirt was heaving wood on the pyre. I wondered if the iron made his skin blister from the horrible heat.

The lighthouse master held his arm out so we would go no further. He pointed up toward a huge round mirror. It was polished glass, curved like a shallow bowl, but much clearer than the dome over King Alexander. Another man in protective clothes was turning it slightly.

To my delight, I could see a moving picture in the mirror. It was as clear and near to me as my hand. I saw blue ocean. A boat was sailing up and over the swells, the waves cresting in white foam. A seagull hovered above the mast. This was a trireme, a swift warship with three banks of oars on each side. I quickly looked out the window in the same direction, but saw only blue.

"Princess," Neva shouted, "it is the magic mirror, the one Olympus told you about."

O, it was a magic thing. To see something up close that was really so far away. So this is one of the machines our astronomers discovered.

The pleasure of seeing this for myself is hard to put into words. Above all, I was comforted for I had seen no royal flag on that ship and the oars were merely wood, not tipped with silver. This meant my father, the king, was not aboard. He was still somewhere on land.

27 FEBRUARIUS

Word has just come.

The messenger who delivered the tablet was an Ethiopian boy, about six years old. He bent so low he tipped over and tumbled at my feet. He started to cry with fear as Neva helped him, poor little one. I kept my royal stance, but smiled at him when he looked up. No doubt he had been trained that when he bows, his neck is at the mercy of Cleopatra's sword. But I do not like to carry weapons, they are heavy and put snags in my dress.

I wave the guards off so the boy could back out of the room unharmed.

Carrying the tablet over to the window where it was light I broke the seal, untied the string, and read Olympus' message:

He had seen my father after weeks of hiding. King Ptolemy and his loyal advisers had finally sneaked back to Alexandria and were in the harbor, ready to sail for Rome. He wrote:

> *Hurry Cleopatra, but beware: Do not eat or drink. Friends of Tryphaena have been hired to poison you.*

Quickly I rubbed out his words and motioned to Neva. Now we must hurry. I will write later about this day.

15 MARTIUS
ABOARD KING PTOLEMY'S SHIP

We have been at sea for ten days. Neva, ill as she is, has cared for me like a sister and reads to me whenever I ask. Dear one! Now she is sleeping below at my insistence.

I, too, have been ill from the constant rolling of our ship. What looked beautiful from the top of Pharos Lighthouse now seems gray and cold and unfriendly. I wish I felt better. I am also nervous. Pirates were seen the other day hiding in the cove of a small island, but we outran them. Our helmsman ordered our royal purple sails to be replaced with white ones, like those used by common fishermen, until we reach safe harbor near Rome.

It is the Ides of Martius, as the Romans call the middle of this month. I curse their sea god, Neptune, for such a rough voyage. Is he under the waves, pushing us up with his arms or is he quarreling with our god Poseidon? Wherever they are, I wish they would afflict someone else.

During the long days, our oarsmen pull and pull as our

boat climbs the waves, breaks through the curling tops, slides down into the troughs, then up again. Hour after hour after hour. Finally I am used to the drumbeat that helps the slaves keep time. At night the drum stops so they can sleep and let the wind work the sails.

The sun is out, but I'm still wrapped in a cloak because of the breeze. Low clouds sit on the horizon, gray with black downward streaks — it feels as if a storm is waiting for us. I write this sitting against the mast, a sail overhead is stiff with wind. My brave man Puzo is doubled over the side emptying his stomach out onto the waves. Even gladiators like Spartacus are said to feel weak at sea. I will give him privacy and turn my eyes to this paper.

The first sheet of papyrus I started writing on earlier today was ruined when a wave struck the bow and poured onto the deck. I had to quickly jump up, but my papers and my dress were already soaked.

I will try again on this dry piece.

Before sunset

Our last night in Alexandria was chaos. My heart is heavy over something that happened with my sweet Berenice.

I had just finished reading the warning from Olympus when a terrible scream filled the palace. My heart beat wildly. *Where is Puzo? Should I hide?* Neva peered out of our chamber, then pointed down the hall. Blood was streaked along the marble, a narrow wet path that led to a courtyard.

O Isis, someone has been murdered! I pressed my hand against my heart to still its pounding. *Am I next?* I wondered.

Tryphaena appeared with three of her Nubian guards. Their black skin glistened with oil, their swords clanked against the bronze ornaments on their skirts. When she pointed at me I stopped and held up my hands.

"What is it, Sister?" I asked. *Say calm,* I told myself. The sight of her angry face, I admit, filled me with terror. *This is the sister who wants me dead. Would she be so bold as to have me killed here, now?*

"When I catch that cat of yours," she said, "I will deliver it to you with its head on a platter." Before I could ask questions, she had spun around and gone out through the atrium. Though she was out of sight, I still felt fear and ran down the hall to Berenice's suite.

I found her on her bed, weeping. She sat up and

grabbed my shoulders. Black eye paint streaked her cheeks.

"Did you do it on purpose?" she asked.

Then she told me. She had been in her chamber playing with Baboon on the Persian rug where I now stood. Berenice went into the next room to find a toy when she heard her pet shriek, as babies often do when their mothers leave.

Berenice took no notice until the shrieks grew louder. She returned to see a leopard in the doorway, crouched low, stalking the little monkey. While Berenice screamed for help, my Arrow (yes, my bad cat) pounced on Baboon and carried it away in her jaws, disappearing out into the garden.

I grieve over the fate of Berenice's little pet, but I think in my heart that a leopard is a leopard whether it walks through a jungle or palace.

As the night grew late, Neva, Puzo, and I hid ourselves on one of the roof gardens, safe inside a tangle of vines. From here, we could look down into the main courtyard and see Tryphaena and her guards every time they passed an open hallway. She was searching for me, I believe. We tried to remain perfectly still, without a breath or rustling of leaves, for I did not want her to find us. When I saw some of her guards row out to my island palace, I thanked Puzo in my heart for not letting me hide there.

From the roof garden we also watched the harbor. At last, we saw a torch being waved from the jetty and knew Olympus was signaling us. Puzo hurried with us out into the dark streets to the docks where ships from the royal fleet were casting off. He jumped onto the boat then reached over the water to grab us as we leaped aboard. My heart was beating so fast I had no breath to thank him.

When Father first saw me the next morning he was shocked.

How did we find him and why were we here? he asked. He was steadying himself against the rail, the rolling sea at his back. I was still dressed in a brown chiton. (Neva was below, unpacking our chests that had been sneaked aboard days earlier.) I explained there were schemes against my life, not just his, and how Olympus helped me escape.

"I want to be with you, Father," I said. "When you meet Caesar, two Ptolemies will be stronger than one."

He looked at me with tired eyes and took both my

hands in his. Smiling sadly, he said, "Daughter, you are as brave as Nefertiti."

My heart soared. Does he know how I admire Nefertiti? In my jewel box I keep a brooch, with the carved profile of this beautiful queen who lived more than a thousand years ago. During my many hours in the Library, I have studied her greatness and that of her husband, Pharaoh Akhenaton. Their religion was based on worshiping one god only, the Spirit of Truth. Some Egyptians hated them so much for this, they destroyed monuments and erased their royal names from many of the records. I am honored that Father thinks I resemble Nefertiti in character. She stood strong for what she believed and did not worry about what others thought of her. I will write more on this after my stomach settles. I am feeling ill again.

To continue . . .

Our ship is among a small fleet of royal triremes with Father's servants, advisers, and other loyal officials. He is the commander, but unfortunately he is sleeping again. He is sick not only from the sea, but also from wine. As the days draw near to when he will face the Romans, his courage flees. They might laugh at him or kill him. As he takes pleasure in drink, he prays to his god Dionysus that they will still be our friends and will sail back with us to Alexandria with soldiers.

It is nearing sundown. The northern coast of Africa is on our left, our port side. Desert mostly. A thin strip of white appears to be waves breaking onshore. They must be huge if we can see them at this distance.

A shout has come from one of the sailors climbing the mast! A ship is rapidly approaching from behind.

The next morning

There was no small commotion as Puzo rushed me below the forward deck for safety, in case of pirates. I ducked under the low timbers and noticed Father lying in a berth, passed out with vomit on his chin. I love him, but how can he rule if he is drunk so often? Am I wrong to think that I am the most capable royal aboard this ship?

Another guard threw a cover over Father's head so he would appear to be just one of our drunk sailors, while Puzo tucked me inside a hot little closet filled with coiled ropes. It was horrid. I strained to hear what was happening on deck above and wished I had my hourglass to see how much time was passing. Finally a thump against our hull told me the other boat had caught up to ours and was tying on.

I waited, expecting sounds of fighting, but instead heard the low murmur of men talking. I unlatched the door to my closet and crept out. A fresh breeze flowed down the stairway, along with it a voice I recognized.

Olympus!

The boat's rocking made it impossible for me to run up the steps, so I clung to the railing and pulled myself up. I could see that our pilot had turned us into the wind so we could raft up to our visitors without sailing away. Since we were not moving forward our ship bobbed in the tall swells, tipping far to the left then far to the right. I struggled against dizziness.

O, my heart took delight in seeing Olympus. He held on to a line, his feet spread to balance himself. His smile betrayed our friendship, but his words were solemn.

"Princess Cleopatra," he read from a scroll, "your sister Tryphaena wishes you to know that because you and your father are fleeing to Rome she is now queen and pharaoh.

If either of you ever set foot in Egypt, you will be executed immediately."

So it was true. Tryphaena had wanted me dead. Her loyal friends must have been singing songs about me in the streets and writing those murderous notes. I wonder which mummy's grave she had robbed to get the skull that had been put in my palace on Antirrhodus.

Olympus glanced at me. He stood bravely, but he swallowed hard with this terrible report. He and I both knew that if I returned to Alexandria I was doomed. If I stayed away to save my life, he and I would never see each other again. If he sailed with me now he, too, would be banished, never again to see his own family.

"Father is ill," I said to the two officials with Olympus. "I will give him your message. Thank you."

O, my heart ached at that moment. I wanted to be alone with my friend, to have one of our long, quiet talks, but already he was lowering himself over the side, down the rope ladder. The messenger ship that had brought him was a small swift vessel with slaves rowing double-time and in shifts through the nights.

Wait, I wanted to cry to Olympus. Instead I grabbed the side of my chiton so I wouldn't trip and went down below. A guard followed me but I waved him off. "I wish to be alone with my father," I told him.

I went to his bunk and removed the blanket from his head. A waterskin hung against the wall, which I poured onto a cloth that Neva handed me. She sat on the floor next to me as I washed Father's face, all the while telling him about Tryphaena, how she is like a spider waiting in his web.

He slept on. With a sadness I could not yet understand I lay my head on his chest and wept.

"Father," I whispered, "what will we do?"

My heart was also grieving for Olympus . . . would I ever see him again?

28 MARTIUS

The days seem long. Father did not take the news about Tryphaena well.

Neva helps me practice Latin by reading the poems of Catullus to me. It is quite possible that I will need to speak to the Roman senators myself if Father does not recover. My accent is rough, I am sure. Suddenly the thought of coming face-to-face with Julius Caesar makes me tremble. I am just a girl! For me to ask him to send soldiers to

Egypt and pay all expenses for such a campaign will take a boldness I do not yet feel.

I dare think that much of being a princess is being an actor.

This morning a shout came from our lookout. He had seen an Egyptian grain vessel coming toward us, apparently on her way back to Alexandria. I and others on our boats have been hurriedly writing notes. I have been considering Tryphaena's threat. Because Father will not discuss this I have taken it upon myself to send a message to her from both of us. Soon I will explain my strategy to him.

If the weather is not too rough, passing ships always try to exchange letters to deliver when they arrive in the next port. At this moment, the Egyptian grain vessel is dropping her sails, and we are dropping ours so we can approach each other slowly. Just below her bow is a figurehead of the twin gods Castor and Pollux, who appear to be dancing as the ship rises with each wave. The figurehead is painted gold, red, and royal blue, one of the most elegant carvings I have ever seen, perhaps because sailors believe these gods will protect them.

LATER . . .

Well, it is done. Our sails are up again. We now have a pouch of their letters bound for Sicily and Rome, they have ours. I am cheered to think that in two weeks Olympus might be reading mine.

> *Princess Cleopatra, aboard the royal ship Roga, in the Mediterranean Sea, to Olympus, scholar and trusted friend:*
>
> *Mercy to you and peace. Deliver the attached letter to my sister Tryphaena, please. I have told her she may remain queen, that Father and I will submit to her authority and be her humble servants if we return to Egypt. Perhaps if she does not fear us, she will let us live.*
>
> *I await to hear from you, dear friend, when the next ship from Alexandria brings letters to Rome. If you find Arrow take her, please, to the zoo. She will be safe with the other leopards there. Bucephalus is surely doing well in your care.*
>
> *And does the terrible snake still hide in the palace? If Isis favors me, she will lead that serpent to Tryphaena.*

To continue . . .

The seas are calm. No wind fills our sails today so we move slowly. When I look over the side, I can see the long wooden oars swinging up out of the water, their silver tips dripping, then swinging back down into the swells. Over and over and over. The row master sits below, beating his drum to a rhythm that rarely changes. His hourglass hangs from an overhead beam so he knows when to pass around the water bag. Often he sings, sometimes the slaves join in. When the wood begins to creak, he pours olive oil into the leather straps holding the oars in place, to lubricate them. I have noticed this must be done at least once a day.

I do not like to watch these men, for unlike my household slaves, these live in miserable conditions. Their ankles are chained at all times to keep them from diving overboard and trying to swim away. Because this ship has three levels of oars, the rowers must sit inside the hull on benches, one bench on top of the other. Their arm movements must not vary by even an inch or their oar will hit one of the others, causing the ship to veer off course.

A sound I often hear, but close my heart to, is the crack

of a whip over these men's backs. They are beaten often, especially for falling asleep at the oar.

On another subject, the water is so clear I can see barnacles on the sides of our ship. A fish with large black wings appears from time to time just beneath the surface, as if it is our companion. It is as wide across as I am tall, and it uses its wings as if it were a bird. Sailors are trying to catch it to see if it will taste good.

Last night brought sounds from the different ships in our fleet. The god Dionysus is being worshiped daily. This I know because of the crude songs and wild laughter. There is much tossing of the dice, too. Brawling sailors have been rolling empty amphorae overboard, which is foolish because these storage jars are valuable and we would have been able to refill them at the wineries in Rome. I plan to put a stop to this waste.

From one of the ships I heard moaning, loud moaning. Neva and I leaned over the side hoping to hear better. *Someone must be ill or injured,* I thought. But our captain said no. It was just the lioness and her cubs, caged beneath one of the decks. He said there is also a young giraffe, deliveries for Caesar.

30 MARTIUS

We have come to an island called Malta, far north of the African coast. Our fleet is anchored in a bay so everyone can rest and bring aboard fresh fruit and meat. The water is beautiful, clear emerald green; when I look over the rail I can see down to the white sandy bottom. Schools of colorful fish dart here and there. To our amazement, we also can see the remains of a ship lying on its side, her mast broken in half. The bottom is littered with vases and amphorae, probably once filled with wine or olive oil from Rome. I wonder if the ship and her crew perished in a storm. Certainly, any slaves in chains would not have survived.

The wreckage appears to be shallow enough that we could jump into the water and walk on the soggy remains. So I instructed some of my men to swim down for a closer look, for there could also be treasure or valuables.

Neva and I watched from the bow as three sailors dove overboard. They swam down and down and down and still had not reached the bottom. I had counted to fifty when two of the men suddenly began swimming back up to the surface. As they gasped for air I continued to watch the other man still down there. Gradually he stopped moving his arms and legs. I am sorry to say that by the time I shouted for someone to go in after him it was too late. The poor man had sunk even deeper and could not be reached.

By royal decree I have now forbidden anyone from our fleet to dive for treasure. Perhaps Neptune and Poseidon want to keep it for themselves.

This morning Father's guards rowed him to shore in the little lifeboat, and he is now sleeping on the beach in the warm sunshine. The island is inhabited with a light-skinned people with brown eyes and brown hair, friendly, but not curious about our royal flags. Their language is similar to Latin, but hard for me to understand so we just smile and gesture to one another. As I reflect, it is possible that some of them are descended from shipwrecked sailors.

Puzo is suffering with a bad cold so I have given him the day off to rest.

Thus Neva and I spent the afternoon by ourselves. The waves are small, just to our ankles, and perfect for swimming but I wanted to do so without Father's guards staring at me. These men are tall Dinkas with ebony skin, quite strong. I am thankful they are here to protect us, but sometimes I just want to be alone. Finally, they agreed to sit on the rocks a distance away.

Neva and I held hands to wade in up to our waists. Our chitons floated up like sails. I wanted to swim far out, like the big fish with wings, but was afraid my dress would pull me down.

"Princess," said Neva, "let us wait to swim off the boat, without these long dresses. It will be safer, please." She pulled my arm toward shore.

O Isis, forgive me. All I could think about today was how tranquil it is here. Not once was I afraid for my life or worried about spies. I did not have to whisper my thoughts to Neva, we just spoke out loud like commoners. I could stay on this restful island forever; take care of Father, nursing him back to health; coax Olympus to move here with his family. We could all live in peace even if Alexander the Great does not rise from his tomb.

Would it be so terrible to be a princess in exile?

Evening

This afternoon the little giraffe died. It was taken ashore and buried above the beach. The islanders crowded around, having never seen an animal with a long, spotted neck. Neva and I watched the funeral from the boat, where we sat on deck drying off from a swim.

"The giraffe missed its mother," she said while brushing my hair. "At least now it will not have to suffer being away from home. Yes, Princess?"

"Yes, it is so, Neva." I held up my mirror so that I could see her face next to mine. There were tears in her eyes. Suddenly I felt ashamed. She misses her own mother and I never noticed before.

During dinner, sailors reported to me about a discovery on the island. Among the temples, they saw massive stone carvings of women in pleated skirts — something they had never seen before. They do not know if the carvings are of goddesses or portraits of a queen and her servants. In any event, the statues have been nicknamed the Fat Ladies because they show plump women with enormously fat legs.

The sailors also said that when they were on the western side of Malta, cooking breakfast on the beach, they could see the little island of Goza, just one mile offshore. They were afraid to explore it though because an old legend says that the sea nymph Calypso lives there in her cave. She is the one who lured Odysseus from his ship and made him her prisoner of love for seven years. (I have had Neva read this story to me many times.)

I do not know why my sailors are so frightened. Perhaps they think Calypso is a twelve-foot tall Fat Lady.

2 APRILIS
ON THE ISLAND OF MALTA

Nightfall, still anchored in the bay.

I am on deck, writing under a lantern hung from the mast. As the boat rocks gently on the swells, the light swings left then right, moving shadows across my paper. I can hear the pleasant sound of waves breaking on the beach then receding with a hiss.

Peaceful. That is the only word I can find to describe this day. And were it not for the loud sailors, it would be bliss.

Earlier I penned an order to our fleet, forbidding

drunkenness, but as I was sealing the tablet with wax, Father rose from below deck. He was dressed in his elegant purple robe and carried his reed flutes. He plays these pipes when drunk, thus people mock him with his nickname Auletes, which means "the flute player." For a king, this is not wise.

"Daughter," he greeted me, smiling, but that was all he said before climbing overboard, down to the lifeboat tied up alongside us. His guards rowed him ashore where a party awaited. Royal pennants flew above the banqueting table, torches were planted in the sand like many candles.

I rubbed out my words and slipped the tablet back into my writing chest. How can a princess give an order if her father, the king, has no intention of obeying?

THE NEXT MORNING

It is nearly dawn. Neva and I stayed on deck all night, wrapped in blankets for I wanted to watch the stars. The freedom to be out in the open without fear gave me such gladness of the heart I could not sleep. She and I talked long into the night. I forget how many times we turned the hourglass. I imagined this is the way common sisters

are, sharing secrets and dreams, as sisters who are not com-
peting to be queen. (To honor Neva, I will not write of the
dear things she confided to me.)

Just moments ago I heard the sound of oars splashing
in the water so we looked toward shore. Through the gray
morning light, I saw a small boat being rowed this way, a
lantern in its bow. Now it has pulled alongside, and two
guards are lifting my father, the king, up to the deck. His
hair and robe are wet as if someone poured an amphora
over his head.

I cannot make myself rush to his side! He will not rec-
ognize me or respond as a father should — and he stinks!
The guards are looking at me with questions. O, curses.

LATER . . .

Now that Father is put to bed I can continue. When the
guards did not know what to do with him, I wanted to
shrug or otherwise act like a girl of twelve. Quickly I
thought in my heart that if I am to be queen I must begin
to act like one. How would Nefertiti respond?

Thus I hurried below to straighten Father's cushions.
Neva returned with a pitcher of warm water taken off the

brazier, and together we washed his hands and face, then his muddy feet. He whispered tender words to me as we covered him with a silk sheet and propped up his head. It will be hours before he shakes off the fumes of wine.

"Do not worry," I told him. "I will help you with the Romans, and they will help us with Tryphaena. Do not worry anymore. Sleep now."

Two days later

Now once again we are at sea, heading north to the great island of Sicily. True, just days ago my thoughts were far from this course. I was content to live out my life on a beautiful, quiet island. But reason has returned to me.

I must be brave and think of my country. The peasants along the Nile need a ruler who cares about them. If Father himself cannot care, then I will stand beside him and show him how.

Most important though, my father's throne is at stake, as is the future of Egypt. If he is not careful, if he is not wise, our country could fall under Roman power. Caesar would plunder our riches and parade my family in his arena. Terrible things happen to royalty who are no longer royal.

To continue . . .

We have just sailed past Syracuse, the town in Sicily where Puzo was born, our flags and purple sails once again adorning our lines. While anchored there, I gave him a day to visit his old grandmother. She was so proud to see him on a royal Egyptian ship she stood on the beach and covered her face with her wrinkled hands, weeping.

I gave her a present, a small carved box with a necklace inside: turquoise stones set in gold. At this she started to cry again.

"Princess, this is too much for me to receive."

I took her hand and closed her fingers around the necklace. "But, madam," I said, "it is not too much for me to give." Then, impulsively, I invited her to come live with us in the palace at Alexandria. The grandmother stood straight up with a dignity common to those who toil hard under the sun.

"Thank you, Princess, but I cannot leave my garden or my three sisters."

Thank the gods that I understood her Latin and she understood mine. Then I thought in my heart about this woman's humble life and felt honored to have met her. Now I understand why her grandson is my favorite guard. He is the fruit of her goodness.

Our pilot says we should see the southern tip of Italy in a day, depending on the winds, a report that pleases me because this rolling ocean is wearing me out. Now I have to turn my thoughts to the task ahead. There is business to do with the Romans, and I must not appear to be merely a spoiled princess. I must honor my father yet be ready to speak wisely if his mind fails him.

This morning at breakfast with him, my heart told me, *Yes Cleopatra, a princess you must be.* Father and I were eating melons on deck, in the shade of a blue silk canopy, for the days are getting warmer. I tried to talk to him about Julius Caesar, but on and on he spoke about his favorite subject: himself! Memories of his twenty-three years as king are as fresh as if they happened last night.

To my shame, Father described his most pleasurable days, festivals, and banquets! Thinking I could draw him into history, I asked what he thought of Egypt's Great Pyramids and the Sphinx, for he sailed up the Nile some years ago. I asked if he would like to visit the Great Long Wall of Ch'in, or the Acropolis in our ancestral country. His response?

He yawned!

My father has as little imagination as my sister Berenice. *O gods, forgive them.* How can I shake him into caring about our people or the world around us? By no means do I think he lacks intelligence, but he is not a man who reflects on significant things. For a king, this is a disgrace.

Though he has told me many times that I am his favorite daughter, the affection I felt for him as a child is growing cold. This saddens me.

I know I am young and have much to learn. That is why I study royals from the past, because I can follow their examples. The Queen of Sheba so desired in her heart to have knowledge, that she rode by caravan all the way to Jerusalem to meet King Solomon, the wisest man on Earth. Queen Esther of Persia saved her Jewish people from slaughter by bravely standing before King Xerxes. Nefertiti, she, too, was brave. These queens were once as young as I am now, and they didn't have a Library or Mouseion in which to study. I am most fortunate.

Sunset

Earlier this afternoon a sailor shouted from the top of a mast, "Land!" Now we are running with the wind, tacking through the swells along a rugged shoreline. Directly ahead is a narrow channel that will allow us to sail between Sicily and Italy into the Tyrrhenian Sea. The water is extremely rough. The sailors are terrified and are crying out to their gods, Castor and Pollux, because they believe the whirlpool Charybdis is here, the one that pulls ships to the bottom of the ocean. Homer also wrote of this in his poem about Odysseus.

Before I had time to work myself into a fright, we had sailed through, and there was Italy on our starboard side. *O Isis, at the sight of this country, my heart dropped.* My tranquillity has fled! What folly to think I am prepared to face the fierce Romans.

I stood in the bow to feel the breeze coming off the land, to once again smell flowers and trees. The motion of the ship rising in the waves reminds me of riding Bucephalus, her fast smooth canter. (O, how I miss her.) I looked down into the water, and my heart filled with gladness to see dolphins leaping alongside our ship, keeping pace as if they were escorting us. Is this our reward from Poseidon and Neptune for enduring a rough voyage?

I am moving my pen quickly across this page because we will soon arrive. Neva and Puzo have been cleaning Father up, helping his assistants see to his wardrobe, then they will raise our pennants and flags. Fishing boats have been approaching. One pulled close enough for a man to shout at <u>me</u>, for he knew by our sails that an Egyptian princess was aboard.

Puzo stepped in front of me protectively and would not let me peer around him to answer. This barbarian said something so coarse, so cruel I cannot repeat it here. I wanted to cast a rope around his thick neck, but Puzo hurried me down below. Is this a warning of what awaits us? *O Isis, help!*

Ever since I can remember I have applied my mind to learning, but somehow I failed to learn that the city of Rome is <u>not</u> a seaport, but lies inland some sixteen miles up the Tiber River. Our ship was guided safely to the mouth of this river by the lighthouse at the walled city of Ostia. After nearly three weeks at sea, O, my heart leaped when I saw it, such a familiar comfort from home. It is not nearly as tall as Alexandria's, but its bright flame made me feel welcome. It, too, sits on a rocky point of land.

I noticed beautiful villas along the coast, which are summer homes for the wealthy. Our pilot pointed these out to me, then steered around the lighthouse into a bay that was busy with merchant ships newly arrived from other islands and parts of Italy. The water was choppy with so many oars churning back and forth, but it is rough also because this is where the river meets the sea. Both sides of the Tiber were crowded with docks. Cargoes were being unloaded from ships and transferred to wagons because the river is too shallow for sailing.

And so, too, our royal fleet would have to remain anchored in the port of Ostia. While the crews moved our belongings to carts and donkeys, Neva and I rested in a newly planted cornfield. As far as I could see there were lush, green vineyards, neatly laid out in rows, white clouds high overhead. We camped here one night, then early the next morning took off on a side road that runs alongside the Tiber. It was sandy and slow-going, but I quite enjoyed the walk. After so many days at sea, it felt wonderful to stretch my legs.

Imagine my pleasure to see woods and a cool forest

along the way, then meadows with flowers. An oasis in Egypt is as lovely, but it is surrounded by desert. Periodically, on the side of the road, there were stone posts with numbers carved onto them, to mark distances. By these milestones, I was able to know how much further it was to Rome.

Now to mention something unpleasant: The river is <u>foul</u>. At this time of year it is perhaps only two feet deep, flowing like brown oil, bringing from the city all types of disgusting things that float: bloody rags, onions and melons, broken pieces of furniture. A stench hovers in the air for miles. As we finally entered Rome late in the afternoon, I understood why. Houses and shops have been built along the banks of the Tiber, jutting out over the water. I saw women dumping who-knows-what from their windows. There is also a sewer pouring out into the river through a well-built stone arch. On the bank directly above this sewer is the Temple of Hercules Victor — I think worshipers must hold their nose when they present their offerings.

O, I regret my complaints about the ocean, for at least it was clean. Will I sound too royal if I say that I miss the Nile, that I yearn to be near a living river?

15 Maius
Rome

Father says that when in Rome, it is good politics to do as the Romans do, thus we are all dressed in togas. They are heavy itchy things because the linen cloth also contains wool. And the sandals, O, what discomfort. The thick leather straps cut into my feet.

I want to record as many events and sights of Rome as possible, so when I return to Egypt I will not forget. Also, Olympus and Theophilus will ask every detail of me, I know them! So, I begin.

Many of the Romans have sundials in their courtyards. They also use water clocks so they can tell time indoors and when clouds hide the sun. We have these in Alexandria, but I said nothing, not wanting to insult the official who proudly showed us around. (I prefer my hourglass in any event.)

We have been staying at the villa of Tullus Atticus, a wealthy citizen who wants to help Father reclaim his throne. Atticus is a stout bald man, pleasant enough, but he appears bloated, as one who is given to gluttony. The tips of his fingers are stained purple from eating grapes, which he does while being read to. His reader has the deep, cultured voice of an actor, so pleasant that whenever they are in the courtyard together I sit nearby to listen.

His villa is near the stinking river I mentioned earlier, but the rooms wrap around courtyards that are lovely with flowering fruit trees, fish ponds, and fountains. An atrium with an opening to the sky brings light into the entryway. A pool in the center catches the rain, thus there is fresh water for the many cats and puppies running about. The bath in my private suite is similar to home, with hot water provided by an underground fire.

Walls inside the villa are brightly painted in blue, green, and yellow. There also are murals with scenes of the countryside, family members and the like. Pedestals throughout the halls display marble busts of dead relatives. A servant explained to me that Atticus is comforted in his sorrow over the loss of his sister, his father, and an infant daughter, by being able to gaze on their faces. A sculptor comes every year to carve the images of his children and good friends. I think in my heart that Egyptian mummies are not nearly so beautiful or lifelike as these.

Floors are decorated with mosaics, one in the entry depicts a guard dog with snarling, sharp teeth and the word

"Beware." Perhaps this is wishful thinking on the part of Atticus because I have not seen his dog do anything except wag its tail and take long naps in the shade.

Atticus also has many stables. I do love the smell of hay and horses, but so do flies, untold numbers of them. Servants follow us everywhere we go, waving peacock feathers to keep the insects away from our skin. At night when we sleep we are protected by silk bed hangings. Another way the Romans catch bugs is with long strips of paper that are coated with a mixture of honey and resin. These hang from the ceilings so that flying insects bump into them and stick. It is not a pleasant sight, nor smell. Dead bugs stink the same as dead rats.

Yesterday, Father and I toured the city by sedan chairs, as no carriages are allowed in the streets during daylight. We were each carried by four Hebrew slaves who had been captured in Jerusalem by Pompey. I tried not to eavesdrop, but I could hear them talk among themselves. They spoke longingly of the hope they have in their god, who one day will free them from captivity. Perhaps they did not realize an Egyptian princess can understand their language. My Jewish friend Theophilus taught me well.

Like Alexandria, Rome is surrounded by a thick stone wall, built more than three hundred years ago. The city itself is full of cramped apartments built one on top of the other, with several families living in each one. Shops are on the ground floor. There are Senate offices wedged next door to tenements which are next door to marble temples. Such disorder!

And graffiti stains every wall. Some are lines of poetry written in Latin as well as Greek; some are election notices. I saw names of gladiators, even faded notes about the great Spartacus, but much of the writings are vulgar. O, the crude thoughts of man.

How can an imperial city allow such squalor?

In my opinion, the Romans have spent entirely too much effort conquering the world when they should sweep their <u>own</u> front step.

We have not met Julius Caesar. I had thought he would be on the docks when our ships arrived in Ostia, ready to receive us. But he is up north, building catapults and battering rams to conquer more of Gaul or possibly Brittania, people here are vague.

We did meet Pompey the Great.

16 Maius

Our third night here, Atticus held a banquet in our honor. Neva helped me dress in a fresh white toga with a sachet of myrrh tucked next to my skin. She painted my toenails blue then fastened delicate gold chains with tiny bells around my ankles. I wore a crown of henna blossoms, my hair brushed straight to my shoulders, my eyelids also painted blue.

I wanted to appear royal, but not cheap like Berenice. Neva held up my mirror for one last look, then we walked outside. We followed a path lit by tiny oil lamps that had been placed in the dirt alongside the stones. When we passed the kitchen, I saw a long fire pit where several wild boars were roasting on spits, other meats were turning, also ducks and small fowl.

The banquet hall was a grand room that opened on to gardens, reminding me of home. Couches had been arranged around low tables, so that three of us could recline together while eating. Pillows and covers are in the same colorful fabrics we have in Alexandria, I suppose because we trade with the same countries.

I leaned into one of the cushions and tucked my feet

under my dress. As soon as I did, a serving girl appeared. She set before me a simmering dish of small roasted songbirds arranged quite beautifully with asparagus tips and spotted quail eggs, cooked in their shells. Red grapes were piled in the center of the table like Mount Vesuvius, surrounded with plates of figs and large green olives. So much to eat!

As bowls and platters were moved about, I noticed the tablecloth was stained from many meals past, crusted with dried foods and vomit. In my royal opinion, it was a disgusting way to offer a meal, but I said nothing.

Eventually, slaves brought to Father and me flasks of water to pour over our fingers so we could wash between bites, while someone held a bowl under our hands to catch the drippings. I was grateful for this because the little birds were greasy and I did not want to wipe off my fingers on the soiled tablecloth or in my hair (like two of the senators were doing).

Father seemed startled when soldiers in helmets and red plumes marched into the room with trumpets. After they played a few piercing notes, General Pompey himself strode in, a red cloak draped over his shoulder (like Alexander the Great!), and thick armbands. He touched the handle of his sword and looked around the room as if he were in a hurry to go somewhere else.

When his hard eyes fell on me I began to shake inside, but I knew I must at least <u>pretend</u> to be brave. I held my head high and could feel my pearl earrings brush my neck as I turned to face him. As princess I will never bow or curtsy to a barbarian, though Neva at my side did so. Puzo stood behind me, I could hear his breathing and a *clink* as one of his bracelets touched his own sword, ready to defend me.

"Well then!" Pompey shouted, clapping his hands over his head. Dancing girls appeared. They wore billowy silk and on the ends of their fingers were tiny brass cymbals. The dancers swayed to the music of tambourines and African drums. In between the tables a family of Pygmies did somersaults; they wore brightly colored harnesses with bells. I felt in my heart that everything was too loud and wild.

TO CONTINUE . . .

As our meal began, Pompey walked over to our table, smiling broadly. When Father stood to greet him, Pompey clasped both his arms and began speaking rapidly in Latin. Father didn't understand one word, but I surely did.

"King Auletes," the general said, "so we finally meet, you gorilla face. Indeed you are half-baked, a decrepit drunk with a nose like a plum. Did our trumpets wake you from your nap, you lazy dullard?" Dropping Father's arms, he turned to where I reclined.

"Ah, little child." He smiled.

O Isis, I can't repeat what Pompey said to me, but the words were as rude and hurtful as the fisherman's who came alongside our ship in the harbor. His words were graffiti on my heart.

Slowly I stood up and looked around me. The soldiers were grinning with pleasure at their leader's clever trick. I thought in my heart that I must be brave and strong, like Queen Esther and the Queen of Sheba who in their day spoke before the most powerful men on earth.

"Sir," I began in Latin, "I am Cleopatra, Princess of the Nile, third daughter of the King and Pharaoh of Egypt, the man you have so cruelly insulted."

At first, I was so nervous my voice trembled. The Latin words felt awkward on my tongue, but soon I was speaking with confidence, quite well, it seems, because the look on Pompey's face was one of shock. His soldiers' smiles dropped like dead flies. I began to relax.

Bless Father! His pale expression had changed to delight and admiration for me. He hadn't understood the words, but he understood the tone.

"General Pompey," I continued. "We come before you humbly to ask your help, but not as fools. If this evening is sport for you and your baboons, to mock the royal family of Egypt, with whom your country has traded precious items for years, just say so. We will return to Alexandria immediately and burden you no longer."

O, I could have gone on and on, but I stopped myself, remembering something Olympus often would say when I talk too much: *The more words, the less the meaning, and how does that profit anyone?*

My heart was pounding so furiously I wanted to stomp out of the banquet hall, but that would have been the temper of a twelve-year-old girl, not the noble response of a princess. As I put my thoughts to what I should now do, Pompey looked directly at me.

"No indeed, Your Highness," he said in a voice soft enough that only I could hear. "You are no fool. Come, let us sup." Thank the gods, I was spared further embarrassment.

But as for Father . . . a different story.

19 MAIUS

Of course, the banquet made Father merry. Even though Romans dilute their wine with water, he still drank too much. He brought out his pipes, which had been tied to the sash of his robe. He played, he sang, he danced, he showed his good manners by belching as loud and often as Pompey. When slaves began to snuff out the torches, to signify the evening was ending, I was pleased that no one had further mocked my father.

In my heart I know they wanted to, but they silenced their jokes knowing that their language was understood by the Princess of the Nile. Also in my heart, I thanked Olympus for teaching me Latin and I thanked Neva for helping me practice during our long ocean voyage.

Back in my chamber I undressed and bathed while Neva read one of Cicero's speeches to me. He was a famous lawyer here in Rome, but is in exile now. When the last grains of sand in my hourglass had dribbled through, I went to bed.

I lay awake for hours it seemed, Neva on the floor mat next to me, Puzo sleeping in the doorway. I could hear the fountain outside my window and the sweet song of a night bird. The wool blanket itched through my cotton tunic, but it was warm at least. I pulled it up over my bare shoulders. A small lamp burning with olive oil flickered in the corner, the smell is unlike the sweet fragrances of my home.

O, I want to go home, I cried silently. *I wish I had my island palace in which to hide.* Hot tears soaked the pillow under my cheek. Standing up to the barbarian Pompey may have seemed natural to those watching, but it left me in pieces inside. He is one of the most forceful, dangerous men in the world. Three years ago he, Julius Caesar, and a rich politician named Crassus seized control of the Roman government. They call themselves the Triumvirate.

Woe to Father! Tonight I learned he is not respected at all. By anyone. This is why I want to go home. My life is not safe here with Romans who laugh at King Ptolemy. It would be easy for them, and probably would give them great pleasure, to feed the two of us to the lions. They then could invade Alexandria, do away with my sisters and brothers, and add Egypt to their empire.

At this moment, my heart is filled with rage at Father because he is not my protector. He is more a fool than I ever realized.

Olympus says knowledge is the way to wisdom, but he did not tell me that wisdom hurts the heart.

To continue . . .

A few days ago a ship arrived in Puteoli, the port south of Ostia, having sailed from Alexandria in a record-breaking twelve days. When I heard that a courier from this ship was racing on horseback to Rome (one hundred miles!), I knew in my heart that there were messages for us. I ran from the villa, down a path to the road. The courier handed me a parcel, somewhat moist from its sea voyage, but dry inside. Letters! Six for Father, two for me!

I broke open the seal on one of mine and read hungrily.

> *Olympus, friend, loyal companion, and student*
> *of medicine in Alexandria, to Princess Cleopatra*
> *in Rome, friend much missed:*
> *Good news. Come home.*

His message was shorter than his greeting! And mysterious. What did he mean? I tucked the other letter in my toga to read later, for at that moment I heard shouts from Father's chamber.

20 MAIUS

For three days, there has been much celebrating.

Tryphaena is dead.

Those letters to Father detailed how, after we left Alexandria, his friends sneaked into the palace while Tryphaena slept, then killed her guards. (In my heart I thought, *What friends?*) Awakened by the commotion, she sat up in bed and screamed for help while putting on her slippers. (An odd thing to do, in my opinion.) But men tied up her arms and carried her through the dark streets to the Gymnasion, where some of our wrestlers were waiting. One of them stood behind her, grabbed her around the neck, then with his strong arms lifted her up until she had strangled. A slipper that had fallen from her foot was delivered to Father as proof.

"Long live King Ptolemy!" each message read.

No word was given about Berenice, if she lives, dies, or if she has been put in chains.

My heart did not miss a beat when I heard the report about Tryphaena. During one of my many debates with Theophilus, he said that God Almighty created men and women in his image. If this is true, I argued, then surely Tryphaena has a good side if only we look hard enough.

"Maybe so, Cleopatra," he said, "but can the Ethiopian change his skin or the leopard its spots? Neither can they do good who are accustomed to doing evil." He and I and Olympus once spent hours reasoning together on this subject, but in the end they both agreed I would never be able to trust Tryphaena. Now that she is dead I need worry no longer.

And yet . . . her murder means it would be even easier for the Romans to conquer Egypt. All they would need to do is quickly kill Father and me. This thought makes me frantic to leave Rome . . . now! While we are still alive.

I asked Father if Tryphaena's death means we can return to Alexandria.

"Oh, yes, Daughter, soon." His eyes were clear, he looked alert. I enjoy my father when his high spirits are from good news, not good wine. But I do not think he understands the danger we are in.

Thus, I was quiet when we spoke to Atticus. In his

citizen's toga with his plump white arms he looked like an imperial rich man. We stood in an office of his villa as a scribe wrote down everything that was said. In my heart I believe Romans do not care about us, or who is on our throne. To them, Egypt is merely another province waiting to be seized by their empire. I knew this was true by the way Atticus shrugged his fat shoulders at our report, his big loose lips turned down with boredom. Pompey, too, was casual. He slapped Father on the shoulder and opened his mouth to laugh. A few Latin words tumbled out — I will not repeat them here — but he glanced my way and took a respectful tone.

"Friends," he said, "we will sup tonight when the moon rises."

I have been in my chamber resting from the day's excitement. Tonight is another banquet, a celebration. In my heart I worry that Atticus and Pompey might be planning to kill Father and me.

TO CONTINUE . . .

Now I sit at the table by my bed. I must think carefully how to tell Father what I have just learned.

Neva was pouring hot water into a basin for me as I unwrapped my toga and lay it on a bench. A letter fell to the floor, the one I had forgotten about. Turning it in my hand, I saw the seal was from a student at the Mouseion: Theophilus!

I opened it with happy anticipation, as one who is about to eat a sweet. Theophilus was always pleasant with me, and eager to share something he had just learned, especially if it came from one of the scrolls of his Torah. My eyes fell to the middle of his letter, which he had written in Hebrew, to the words "Berenice has crowned herself queen." Then I started at the beginning, reading the entire letter several times before I understood.

Apparently of all the messages delivered to us today, Theophilus' was the last written, the last to be hurried aboard the ship leaving for Rome. He reported this:

Hours after Tryphaena was strangled, Father's few friends who had seen to the deed were, unfortunately, too wise in their own eyes. Congratulating themselves with wine, they soon fell into a stupor. Immediately they were attacked by Berenice's guards, killed with flying swords.

Now <u>Berenice</u> sits on Father's throne! I tried to see her in my mind. Was she haughty and proud of her new role? I did know she would enjoy our dead sister's wardrobe and jewels. I wonder if she has acquired another monkey. And is she now married, as is expected of Egyptian queens?

Woe to Berenice. I am frightened for her. She is too bland and timid to stand up to Father when he returns. Did she forget the Romans would be coming, too?

EVENING, AFTER SUNSET

Father took the news calmly. After meeting again with Pompey, all is as originally planned. As soon as soldiers can be gathered our fleet will set sail, Roman warships escorting us.

In my heart I wonder if I can trust this plan. Another worry is that, though Father adores me, he is unpredictable. What if the next time he is drunk, he gets it in his head that I, his third daughter, am trying to seize his throne? His officials would kill me.

At times I feel so burdened by these worries.

During the meeting last night I sat on a stool next to Father. We heard someone walking toward us through the long hallway. I knew it was a soldier, because of the clicking his boots made against the marble, for all military sandals have iron hobnails in the soles. He entered the room smiling, his helmet tucked in his arm. Over his tunic he wore the brass belt of an officer with an apron of leather strips decorated with pendants. These ornaments fell to his knees and made a jangling noise with every step he took.

He saluted by placing his right fist over his heart then raising it toward Pompey. I was quite taken by this soldier's robust looks and his cheerful manner. Introductions went around. I pushed my stool back to stand and say my name, but I was not going to bow to him.

"Marc Antony," he responded, smiling at me, "and I am enchanted, Your Highness." He said something else in Greek, but his accent was so rough I didn't understand him.

An official standing behind me whispered that Antony, though Roman, was born in my city, Alexandria. He is about twenty-six years old and is the chief cavalry officer who will lead the soldiers to Egypt, to restore Father to the throne. He seemed so merry I could not see in my mind how he might wield a sword against enemies. Was he to be my protector?

I looked at him directly. In Latin I said, "Is your good cheer from what you drink, Marc Antony, or is it from what you think?"

He threw his head back in laughter. "Clever girl," he said, "but you are just a child to speak so."

O, my temper rose at this. I gave him a cold, hard stare before remembering I must be on good terms with this commander. If he succeeds in deposing Berenice and restoring Father to his throne, then my life in Alexandria will be safe once again. Safe, that is, if the Romans leave us alone. And safe, as long as Father believes I am his favorite daughter, not a competitor.

The sharp words I wanted to say to Marc Antony remained in my head. Thus I was silent. Father broke the tension with a cheerful report on the weather. As the men joined in with other meaningless chatter, I kept my eye on Antony. He had a well-grown beard and a strong face, and I noticed that his laugh brought smiles to those around him, even myself.

After many moments, my heart softened.

To continue . . .

A young woman arrived in a sedan chair. She is a bit older than myself and very beautiful. Her hair was swept up in the style of a noble lady and she wore a white toga with a thin, crimson sash. Her eyes were kind. The way she smiled at me gladdened my heart.

An official introduced her to me as Julia, the bride of Pompey. I was surprised such a sweet-looking girl was married to that man, that vulgar brute, but even more surprised when she said her father is Julius Caesar!

As we visited with each other, slaves brought in goblets of apple nectar so we could refresh ourselves. They also served us bread, sliced thin and frosted with cheese and bits of black olives. A reader stood by the fountain, reciting the latest poem by Catullus who himself lives in a nearby villa.

Well, I'll be brief now, for it is quite late and my eyes feel heavy. Julia's visit was solely to invite me to the theater tomorrow afternoon! I will be happy to see more of Rome and perhaps make a friendship with her.

13 Junius
Still in Rome

So much rain. I've been ill with a terrible cold, so have not recorded my thoughts for some days. Now as I pen this, the hour is late, the house of Atticus is quiet. His reader left an hour ago. For the moment, my companion is a white cat sitting in the doorway that opens out to the garden. It is watching a nightingale drink from the fountain. (O, beware, little bird.)

To continue about my day with Julia . . .

The streets of Rome are as crowded and noisy as Alexandria's. Slaves carried our chairs with a bumpiness that made me grab onto the sides for fear I would tumble out. It would be a messy fall, because the cobblestones are soaked with refuse: kitchen garbage, dung from horses and dogs and most putrid of all, waste from latrines that has been thrown out windows. Stepping stones imbedded in the road are the only way people can cross the street without fouling their feet.

Such wretched air! The sides of my sedan had curtains made of thin blue silk that protected me from splashes and from the eyes of curious men, but the heat was stifling inside. O, to be home again, where the sea breeze is as near as my face.

During our ride through the streets, Puzo jogged alongside me. And to my amusement, so did someone's little muddy pig, which followed us until some boys chased it away. When we arrived at the theater, Puzo's legs were so caked with dung he washed in a public fountain before coming in with me. This theater is similar to the one we have in Alexandria, an open-air stage surrounded by seats that spread upward, giving the appearance of a large bowl.

We were escorted to the front seats, which are reserved for nobles, that is, senators and visiting royalty such as myself. The next twelve rows behind us are for knights, this is what Julia calls the wealthy businessmen (such grand flowing togas and fat chins!).

A servant placed cushions on the stone bench for us. I turned around to look up at the crowds beginning to fill the audience. The steps upward were such a steep climb, my heart was thankful that we were on the ground level.

Soon the play began. It was titled *The Clouds*. It is a Greek comedy written hundreds of years ago by Aristophanes. From where the actors stood, their voices carried clearly to us as well as high up and around the theater, for the audience laughed or hissed at the same times we did. I was lost in enjoyment! The satire was about our great Socrates. But it was so biting, I think if he were alive today he would drive a sword through the writer.

O, it was good to be out. I noticed people staring at me from time to time, as I was in the front row, center, which is the seat of honor. Perhaps they are curious about an Egyptian princess who dresses as a Roman. No matter. Puzo watches carefully for my safety.

The play ended at sunset. On the way home, Julia instructed our servants to carry us down an alley that opened up into a quiet little courtyard. It was lit by a lantern hanging from the branches of an olive tree. Tall walls surrounded us, and I could hear from the apartments above sounds of families ending their day — children being tucked into bed and other noises.

I soon realized we were in a public eating place. We stood at a waist-high table that curved around a charcoal fire. Julia took two coins from a pouch that was tied to her belt and laid them on the bar. She told me that children stop here in the mornings for breakfast before they go sit with their tutors.

The cook put ground meat onto a plate. Several small bowls on a sideboard held salt and other spices. He pinched some of each, then added a fistful of pine nuts to the meat, mixing it together with his hands. Then he patted the meat into two flat disks, each the size of his palm.

From a jar he poured olive oil into a pan that was heating on the coals. The oil spit when he dropped in the meat, then began sizzling. I was quite taken with the delicious aroma. At last, the cook picked the meat out of the hot pan with his fingers then placed it between two slices of bread, handing one to each of us.

We ate standing up. I was so hungry I wanted more, but did not want to impose on Julia. I had not thought to bring coins of my own. As we were climbing into our sedans something splashed near my feet. I looked up to see an open window where someone had just emptied a chamber pot.

Barbarians.

Julia and her guard saw me to the door of Atticus' villa. Thanking her for the lovely day, I asked what our meal was called. It had tasted so good.

"The usual," she said, "fried dormouse."

To continue . . .

Bad news has me in low spirits today.

It seems there are not enough soldiers to escort us to Egypt. Most of the military is far north with Caesar, so now we must wait! We need legions to battle the peasants and those who put Berenice on Father's throne, but it will be many weeks before more men are trained.

In my heart I worry. It is already June. Summer solstice will be soon. From that day forward, the sun's shadows grow longer, the days shorter and cooler. Because the winds favor ships traveling south, it would be possible to journey home in ten days, before autumn, before Poseidon and Neptune throw contrary winds at us. But we must leave no later than early September. The seas are too dangerous after that.

I am sick at heart about this. There are so many things I miss about home. I miss Olympus and Theophilus, our long talks and days of study. Arrow and Bucephalus, what has happened to my pets? Most of all, in this heavy summer heat I miss the ocean breeze.

I am Princess of the Nile, but this evening I do not feel royal. I want to stomp my feet! I fear I will go mad — yes, mad — if I have to stay here through the winter. Woe is me!

After Dinner

Rome is stinking hot. Most of the wealthier citizens have left the city for their cool summer homes along the coast. How I envy them. Though Alexandria has odors, there is always wind off the sea to blow the foulness away.

I have not written about my worries lately. If the Romans are plotting to kill Father and me, and to conquer Egypt, what can I do to stop them? They will do what they do when they want. And my fears about Father's betraying me? I must be kind to him and not give him cause to think I am like my older sisters. True, I want to be queen, but not by any ill deeds. In my heart I wish I could stop him from drunkenness, but what daughter can save her father from this?

Meanwhile, he has been visiting the soldiers in their barracks and watching new recruits learn drills. He meets with senators and prominent citizens to ask for money and help restoring him to his throne. Father wants to have as many Romans on our side as possible.

It seems he is behaving himself, perhaps because he knows he must. After all, he is now king in name only, his throne being occupied by Queen Berenice. She is twenty years to my twelve, and if I know her as well as I think I do, she is probably just putting on displays of fashion and beauty.

I doubt we will ever hear that she has bettered the lives of the Egyptian people or anyone else besides herself. Though she is my favorite sister, my heart has no respect for her. This, too, makes me sad. It makes me want even more to be queen.

On another subject, bad weather is reported. Hail has damaged many of the vineyards and vegetable gardens near Ostia.

15 Junius

It seems that my low mood was reported to Tullus Atticus. To cheer me, he sent a silver plate to my chamber. On it was a letter, his wax seal on the top of the page and this message: *Come, dear Princess, to Herculaneum. A royal suite overlooking the sea awaits you.*

My heart swelled with happiness. Atticus has invited

me to his summer villa on the Bay of Naples, what a kind old baldie. Julia says his place is in a small cove near her own villa. O, joy. Neva is packing, for tomorrow we leave!

This evening when I saw Atticus walking in his garden, I ran to him with thanks. Now I regret the bad thoughts I had toward him.

"Dear girl," he said, "never mind the tears. When you arrive in Herculaneum, spare yourself no expense. My purse is long enough."

23 JUNIUS
IN THE SEASIDE TOWN OF HERCULANEUM

I have been drowsy and content. O, how the sea lulls me. For one week, I have played in the salt water and napped in the sun. Julia says my skin is turning dark, like a commoner's, but I tell her, "And?" (It is so very boring to be royal all the time!) Neva reads to me more often than usual, always ending with the letters I have received from Olympus and Theophilus. As a result, my heart has memorized their words.

Did I mention that the Appian Way goes from Rome to the Adriatic Sea? It was built with large blocks of lava, thus it is black in color, also it is eighteen feet across, wide enough for three chariots to race one another. I mention this only because our caravan came upon a terrible scene. A poor man with a donkey and vegetable cart had been run over and killed by soldiers who had no thoughts but for themselves.

Who drives the fastest chariot should be decided at the race course in the circus, not on a public avenue. If these men had been my soldiers, I would make them give a year's wage to the man's family.

During our journey, I was also distressed by many crosses I saw alongside the road, like tall dead trees. I knew the story. My sisters and I had been told about Spartacus ever since we were little, how he led a slave revolt against Rome that lasted two years. When General Crassus and his armies finally captured Spartacus, Crassus ordered his soldiers to crucify the slaves who had survived battle, six thousand in number.

O Isis! Not until last week when I personally was on this road did I understand. For more than one hundred miles the Appian Way had been lined on both sides with men hanging from crosses. It was a valley of death that would have taken travelers days to pass through. They would have walked under shadows of the dying men.

The slaves' bodies were left there to rot in the sun, as a warning: *Never argue with Rome.*

Even though this happened fourteen years ago, some crosses that remain still have bits of skeleton attached, a hand, a foot. I did see this myself.

Olympus once explained to me in medical terms why crucifixion is the worst of all cruel punishments. After being forced to carry his own cross to the place of execution, the criminal is stripped naked and fastened to the wood with ropes or nails. He hangs by his arms in agony, sometimes for days. Finally, the pressure on his lungs makes him suffocate, it makes his heart burst open.

When Olympus told me this, I remember thinking at the time, only *O*, and then I changed the subject. I knew Romans are the most barbaric people on earth, but so what? They were an ocean away.

How could I have been so insensitive? I wonder in my heart if I will order such torture when I become queen. I think not. O, I hope not. In Egypt, at least our prisoners meet their deaths quickly.

Now indeed, another subject . . . We took this road south to Capua, then turned onto a narrow, rough path that skirted the vineyards on the lower slopes of Mount

Vesuvius. (This is where Spartacus and other runaways had hidden.)

For our entrance into Herculaneum, I kept myself from sight behind the drapes of my carriage. Ours was a royal parade with servants waving flags and colorful silk streamers. Tambourines and singing made all of us merry. I could see through my blue curtains that children lined the road and were running alongside us through the streets. When I slipped my hand out to wave, some excited girls pointed to the jewels on my fingers. These girls were barefoot and wearing short tunics with garlands of ivy in their hair. Their sweetness warmed my heart.

The servants of Atticus had already received word of my arrival, thus all was ready. The rooms were sweetly scented with roses floating in cinnamon oil, bowls of fruit were on the tables, my bed cushions were powdered with spices, all so lovely. And I was happy knowing Julia would be arriving the next day.

To continue . . .

Yesterday was summer solstice, the longest day of the year. Though parties and banquets went long into the night, and there were bonfires at every street corner and all along the shore, I did not join in the festivities. My spirit was low, and I was still weary from our long journey so I stayed in my room. Neva has her own small chamber adjoining mine, Puzo rests in the hallway. My other guards are posted throughout the villa.

I never tire of listening to waves breaking on the beach. My suite faces the bay, and a breeze comes in through a window above my bed. O, how sweet are the sounds and the scent of the sea. This lovely similarity to Alexandria makes me all the more homesick.

All day I've been looking out at the bay. Father promised that his ships will come for me in a few weeks, on their way to Egypt. He also promised that I will not have to return to stinking Rome.

Near midnight, after my large hourglass ran out, I was still too restless to sleep so I stole out to walk along the beach. Breaking waves looked like lines of white foam. In the moonlight I could see a fishing boat anchored in the cove. It moved up and down as the swells rolled under its hull, and there was someone on deck pulling in a long gray net.

The beauty of this evening and the familiar tang of salt

air reminded me so much of home I found myself choked up, yes, crying. I sat in the sand, my arms wrapped around my knees. Would anyone guess this is an Egyptian princess weeping on a Roman shore, weeping from fear and loneliness?

My heart was in torment. There were so many things that could go wrong! What if Father stayed in Rome all summer and his ships never came? What if they did come, but he was too drunk to remember I was here waiting and they sailed past the Bay of Naples without stopping? Something else. He might decide I am a threat to him and deliberately leave me behind, exile me in Italy. O, I tremble at the thought of being abandoned.

For many moments I grieved over this, then finally stood up and brushed the sand from my legs. Suddenly, on a wild impulse, I ran into the water and dove under a wave. O, it was cold! But I felt wonderful, and in an odd way, cleansed of my tears and misery. As I walked along the dark shore in my dripping dress, I made a royal decision.

I, Cleopatra, have no power over what Father does or thinks. I can do one thing and one thing only: wait.

It was then that I noticed a glow in the sky and thought perhaps it was from a lighthouse down the coast. But then

I heard the roar of a crowd and remembered the amphitheater: gladiators were fighting one another tonight.

When our caravan had arrived in town, I saw graffiti painted on the stone walls, with gladiators' names. These had made me smile: *Titus has big arms. He is a heartthrob to young girls. Arcus is a maiden's hero.* Were these men now in the arena?

My own heart felt heavy now, knowing that the cheers meant a man was being killed. Tryphaena loved this cruel sport. She told me she enjoyed the excitement and betting on who would be stronger, lion or man. Because of my youth I have not yet attended such a contest.

Summer, Fifteen days after solstice

This afternoon Julia and I soaked in hot pools that flow up naturally from the ground. We think the water comes from inside Vesuvius because the top of the mountain is often hidden by what looks like steam. No one really knows. I have not mentioned this before, but Rome also has baths from natural hot springs, public ones that are meeting places for senators and knights after they have argued all day in court.

Here in Herculaneum I was thankful that one of the

bath chambers is for ladies only. It had a window looking out to sea, with double panes of glass to let in the light yet keep out the cold air. The glass was thick and blurry, thus it afforded us privacy from the various men wandering along the path outside.

A slave girl came in with a pitcher of cold water and poured it into a basin that stood on a marble pedestal. From this we splashed ourselves to cool off. A masseuse was there to rub oil on my back and shoulders. Then she gave me a strigil, a curved stick made of iron to scrape my skin clean. She offered to pluck the hairs from under my arms as she was doing for other ladies.

"No, thank you," I said. "Not this year, madam."

Father's ships have not come yet. Messengers bring word that new soldiers are training, but still there are not enough to form one legion, a legion having between three and six thousand men. Knowing we are not ready to travel makes me restless, but also I feel a measure of peace because it means Father has not sailed home without me. Meanwhile, vessels from Egypt bring letters from my old friends. I read their words again and again.

Theophilus still writes to me in Hebrew (to keep my mind active, he says!). His report: In the Mouseion, scholars are talking about the steam engine invented some years ago. Now they are trying to put it on a chariot to see if it can roll along without horses. These scholars also were able to make a boat move across the Nile by using steam, but they have decided to abandon the idea.

Do you know why, Cleopatra? It will leave the rowers with nothing to do, and you well know that idle slaves just cause trouble.

His letter caused <u>me</u> trouble in my thoughts. I wish Theophilus were here to observe the Romans and discuss these things with me. If I become queen, will I forbid inventions that allow slaves to sleep all day? I do not know. Ever since Spartacus, people who own slaves have worried about another revolt.

I have just read my other letter, the one from Olympus and now have an ache in my heart. The good news, he says, is the puff adder was found coiled up in a basket, sleeping, and was quickly killed.

But the unhappy news is that Arrow, my loyal leopard, has been missing since the night she ate the little baboon. She has not showed up at the zoo or anywhere in sight of the palace. I suspect Tryphaena's cruelty. Did she do terrible things to Arrow before she herself was killed? Woe!

On another matter, Olympus wrote that Queen Berenice was so bored with her husband that after three days of marriage she had him strangled. Who this man was, I do not know.

LATE SUMMER

I have stopped keeping note of the months for, to me, summer is summer. I live in the blissful knowledge that the sea is out my door. Three wide steps lead down from my terrace to the water's edge. Every day Neva and I swim in the bay. Usually we wear short silk tunics that we belt at our waists so our legs have freedom of movement.

The sea is a beautiful turquoise blue and so clear that when I am underwater my open eyes see fish and tall waving plants that are attached to the sandy bottom.

Around the jetty is another beach where a wealthy nobleman has built public baths within a small cove. Twice a day the incoming tide washes over the rocks, filling the pools with cold, tingly salt water.

It was here that I learned something about Puzo.

To continue . . .

That day Neva and I first swam in the protected pools, then ventured out into the cove itself where bigger waves unfurl onto the beach. Suddenly she was floating away from me on a fast current. In a panic we reached for each other, but our hands slipped apart and she began to be swept out to sea.

I screamed, "Help, someone!"

Her wet hair was matted over her face so I could not see her eyes. But I did see terror in the way her mouth tried to call for help. That was when I noticed Puzo running along the jetty, trying to run faster than the tide. At the outermost tip of land, he threw off his sandals and sword, then dove into the waves that were breaking hard against the rocks.

I saw only his arms above the water as he swam for Neva. Meanwhile my feet had lost touch with the bottom and now I myself struggled in the current. I swam hard for shore. It seemed forever. Eventually I felt a swell under me, pushing me up and over the crest of a wave, dropping me inside the churning foam. I tumbled, choking and swallowing salt water that also rushed painfully up my nose.

At last my feet touched bottom and I dragged myself to shore. Sick with dread, I looked for Puzo.

He was climbing over the rocks with Neva in his arms. He brought her to me, alive. O joy! My heart was touched when I saw the tenderness with which he regarded her.

I knew then that, while Puzo will surely guard me with his life, it is Neva he loves with his heart.

THE NEXT MORNING

Neva and I have both been ill to our stomachs from drinking the sea. I thank Poseidon that he did not pull her down to the depths, but returned her to me safely.

As we rest, Puzo stands in the doorway watching over both of us, quiet as usual, his arms ready to reach for his sword.

My heart feels lonely. How is it that I feel old yet I am still young, nearing my thirteenth birthday? Some princesses are already married by my age, but if for love, I do not know. In fact, I just received a wedding invitation from a daughter in the wealthy Sabinus family, to take place next week in Pompeii, a resort town below Mount Vesuvius. The affair promises to be quite lavish, but the girl's age? Twelve.

As I wrote earlier, I will not betray the secrets Neva has confided in me, but I will say this much. She adores Puzo. She has loved him from first sight. Am I to fear that their affection for each other will diminish their loyalty toward me? Am I to be like Berenice, who forbids marriage between slaves? Should I be coldhearted like Father who will sell a man's bride to a caravan going far, far away?

Or Tryphaena? Her cruelties would be graffiti on this page, so I will not describe them.

I wonder in my heart about Queen Esther and Queen Nefertiti. What would they have done about my two servants? Did the Queen of Sheba ask Solomon about these matters? O, to have their wisdom!

As Neva was brushing my hair this morning I put my hand on hers.

"I am pleased you have eyes for Puzo and he for you," I told her. My heart ached remembering how she had left her family in Greece to serve me. She might never again see her mother or her own sisters. And Puzo, too, was away from his dear grandmother and great-aunts. I never asked him if he would have preferred a gladiator's honorable death to guarding the Princess of the Nile.

I fear asking questions about things I do not want to change.

Neva bowed so that her cheek brushed mine, then she resumed brushing my hair. Her sweetness captured my heart.

Still, I do not know what to do, except keep Father from seeing their love, as much for my sake. If he learns that I approve of their romance, he could put me in chains. Or worse. It is an odd thing to be royal. At times I feel cherished by my father, but at times I worry he will discard me like an old cloak.

It is hot this evening, for the wind is from the east, blowing warm air across the sunbaked vineyards out to sea, blowing off the tops of the waves. My heart is filled with gladness for the generosity of Tullus Atticus who allowed me to summer on the beautiful sea. Surely the dirty heat of Rome would have made me fall into madness.

2 October
Rome again

We have returned to Rome, for now that autumn is near the heat is not as miserable. We have returned also because

Father sent word that he needs me. It seems that while I was in Herculaneum, he was <u>not</u> meeting with Roman officials or seeing to the soldiers as he had promised me. He was seeing to his headaches!

Father's excuse is that meetings are more interesting when I am there. What I think he really means is that people are less likely to mock him, since they know I understand their language.

Forgive me, Isis, but in my heart I mock him myself. Because he has squandered so much time it is now too late to voyage home, for the season of storms is upon us. The rough seas would swallow our ships.

I am so low it feels as if my heart has stopped beating.

My small pleasure is listening to Neva read as I fall asleep. Recently it has been the love poems written long ago by the Greek woman Sappho. The poems are more cheerful than I feel.

26 OCTOBER

After sunset I heard voices in the garden outside my room. I could not help but hear that it was two lovers speaking tenderly to each other — Neva and Puzo! As I write this they have now gone, where, I do not know. *O Isis, do not let Father catch them.*

27 OCTOBER

This morning I called them both to meet with me in the vineyard beyond the kitchen wall. I had been so worried last night that I slept little and was now pacing, speaking in a voice soft enough that only they could hear.

"You must pretend <u>no</u> affection for each other," I told them. "Neva, if Father finds out he will sell you to the Romans. Puzo, he will force you to once again become a gladiator. My father, the king, will tolerate no devotions among his household except to him."

Puzo bowed, his hand on his sword. Neva also bowed. Her hands were cupped toward me in a gesture of thankfulness. They turned for their separate duties, as if the other were not there. What I did not tell them was my own life is in danger if Father finds out.

30 OCTOBER

The days are cool. Rain fills the pools in the courtyards and washes the filth from the streets into the river. Julia said that soon the Tiber will be deep enough for barges to sail right to Rome.

A merchant ship arrived in Ostia last week from Alexandria. It almost sank after having taken on water during a storm, but her mariners lay all their strength to her oars and arrived safely. When vessels have sunk in years past, people have starved from the lack of Egyptian wheat. Julia told me that the greatest enemies of her father, Julius Caesar, are not the Gauls or other barbarians. Winter and famine kill more soldiers than anything.

I mention this particular ship, which now will winter sixteen miles away at Ostia because, not only did it bring grain, it brought food for my soul: letters in Hebrew from Theophilus and letters in Greek from Olympus, my dear friends. Now I wait for spring. Surely by then there will be enough soldiers ready to escort us home.

Meanwhile, I will care for Father who, I am ashamed to admit, needs a nursemaid more than he needs a daughter. I will put my fury aside, for this is my royal duty.

It is also wise politically. I must remain in the king's favor.

SCROLLS 8–11
56 B.C.

12 Februarius

Folly has struck. Woe to me!

Yesterday was the first sunny day in <u>weeks</u>. Neva and I took our clothing trunks outside to our courtyard, to dry out our ever damp dresses and shawls. We draped them over the statues and bushes. (O, we miss the heat and sun of our Alexandria.)

I set Puzo to the task of sharpening his sword, polishing my necklaces, the usual. As he and Neva are literate, they often write notes to each other, which are passed through my willing hands, then destroyed so they might never be read by Father. Thus, their romance remains a stolen glance here and there and whispered conversations when we three sit by the fountain.

Anyone watching will think it is I who am instructing them, rather than the three of us sharing thoughts. It is not the elevated sort that I have with Theophilus and Olympus, but the words exchanged among us are sweet nonetheless, and kind. I am soothed by our hours together.

But I digress. My folly was that while sunning ourselves I brought out my letters and papers to read, where the light was good. I was distracted by the sound of horses approaching up the gravel road and dogs barking. "Hellos" were shouted. I knew the voice of Atticus, but not the other. (Father must have been sleeping again.)

I hurried out, Neva behind me, then Puzo. When I reached the entryway, I dismissed them both for the afternoon.

Our visitor was Marcus Tullius Cicero, a stately man in a toga that was wrapped twice over his shoulder. I had heard of him . . . yes, in fact, Neva has read many of his speeches to me. He is Rome's most famous orator, a lawyer feared in the courtroom by his opponents for his sharp tongue. He had been banished from this city for over a year. The reasons, I don't know, politics perhaps. It seemed curious to me that he was so well dressed because Julia told me whenever a man is banished from Rome he is thereafter forbidden to wear the toga. Maybe Cicero just does as he pleases.

He did not talk about his exile, only mentioning that it had to do with words he said against Caesar's friend. But things are all right between them now.

Introductions were made. I did not bow, of course (nor did he bow to me), but I spoke courtesies to him in Latin, a tongue in which I am now quite fluent. During this meeting I realized we had met before, but I doubt he remembered.

In the summer when I was in Herculaneum, I had just finished a swim and was sunning myself on the rocks. An older man wandered by, waving a long stick of driftwood and talking to himself. He seemed peculiar, for his toga was wet up to his knees and he kept pointing passionately at the ocean. *An odd one,* I had thought.

But now I know this had been Cicero, perhaps practicing an argument that he might give in court. Evidently he was enjoying summer at his villa in Pompeii.

Cicero now took my hand in both of his. "Cleopatra," he said, "that idiot Marc Antony told me a little Egyptian girl is here with us in Rome. Obviously he is a liar for you are no child. You may already know that Antony is usually drunk, therefore, he seems to spew rather than speak."

I like Cicero. Words fly from him like darts. He is near

the same age as my father, but he is not dull or soft. We spent an hour, he and I and Atticus, discussing another play called *The Frogs*. Cicero said he is an active student of Greek literature and tries to keep his mind sharp by memorizing entire works. (I was so interested in this conversation, I did not touch our meal of sardines and olives, nor taste my wine.)

Only when his sedan was brought to the door did I realize it had been raining. He stepped over a wide puddle, holding the hem of his toga to climb up into his chair. Remembering my journal I hurried through the halls to my room. The courtyard was flooded, our dresses were soaked as were my letters. Carefully I peeled apart the soggy papers, hoping to preserve them, but the ink had run. Not one word remained.

My folly was forgetting that in Rome it can rain any time without warning. Thus, the record of my first winter here is lost.

Now, to bed. It is raining once again. The white cat is curled by my feet, a small reminder of my Arrow. I am comforted by its purring.

To continue . . .

More thoughts on Cicero. He visits Atticus often and as I
am an honored guest, I am always invited to join them. I
cannot grow weary of listening to the great Cicero. When
he speaks, he strokes his chin with his left hand as if to
do so helps him think. He is quite glib. He explained the
Triumvirate to me, calling it the Three-headed Monster
because Caesar, Pompey, and Crassus are too hungry
for power.

"They have uncertain tempers," he said, "and I see dis-
aster ahead of all three of them."

Cicero said that I am the first girl with whom he has
enjoyed "Socratic conversation," meaning that we discuss
philosophies and ideas. No trifles or idle gossip. Though
Neva and I do love to whisper such things late at night, I
will not confess this to Cicero.

Morning, first light

I stepped out of bed this morning and almost crunched
underfoot a dead dormouse that the white cat had left for
me. I picked it up by its tail and tossed it outside into a
bush. I am not ready to cook such a creature.

I heard today from Cicero that letters arrived for him from Julius Caesar who is in Gaul securing more Roman territory. It took just twenty-six days because a courier rode as fast as he could, changing horses whenever he found one roaming in a farmer's field.

The courier is resting today before returning to Caesar. Julia and others are writing messages. Am I also to pen something to this man, a chatty hello, perhaps, to get on his good side? Sometimes I do not know if my heart is responding as a royal or a girl of thirteen. Often, so often, I wish my mother were alive to explain things. In the end, I sent him one of my sachets filled with fresh spices.

I have learned more unpleasantness about the richest man in Rome, Marcus Licinius Crassus or, as Cicero calls him, The Crass One.

Already I knew that he was part of the First Triumvirate with Caesar and Pompey. In my heart I call him Crassus the Crucifier because he is the one who ordered the cruelties on the Appian Way.

Well, here is more. Crassus has his own private fire department. *So?* one might ask.

The other evening, Cicero, Julia, and I had just finished

dinner and were taking a walk in the gardens. We saw a glow of light coming from down the street and were curious, of course, so we wandered through an alley until we came to the scene. I will never forget it. A horse-drawn wagon was in the middle of the street, and on this wagon was a large water tank with a pump and leather hoses for putting out fires.

Crassus, the owner of this water wagon, stood nearby with his arms folded over his fat stomach. He was calmly negotiating with a man who was not at all calm, in fact, he was upset and waving his arms because it was his house that was burning.

I crept closer. It was not easy to hear their conversation because of the flames and shouts of neighbors who were panicked about losing their own homes. Crassus wanted the man to pay before he would consider putting out the fire. As the man had no money (it was burning to ash inside his house), he said, "All right, anything!"

This poor man did not realize that "anything" meant he must give his home to the man with the water wagon. Now it is Crassus who owns this property, and the man must pay rent to him for the rest of his life. Julia believes he sets the fires on purpose, because he always seems to be at the scene just in time. I think I know why Crassus is the biggest land owner in Rome.

To continue . . .

Cicero addressed the Senate today. Instead of sitting on the main floor behind the ladies' curtain, I climbed up the circular steps to the gallery. It was crowded with men and women leaning over the bar to hear Cicero present the closing arguments to his case. I was breathless listening to him. Such eloquence. He strides to and fro, gesturing with passion, then he stops dramatically to look at the faces around him. He knows when to speak softly and when to thunder.

Finally, just before sunset, he and the other lawyers met outside and found a way to compromise. Cicero calls this "settling out of court."

The magistrates will be sitting again tomorrow — I plan to listen to Cicero plead as many cases as possible because I want to learn his skills of persuasion. There is another lawyer who intrigues me as well. He wears a blue toga and he paints a black circle around his right eye if he represents a plaintiff, or around his left eye for a defendant. He is quite entertaining because he also pantomimes and leaps about as if he is an actor in a Greek play.

16 MARTIUS

This is my second spring away from home. O, my heart feels so lonesome at times. I have hopes that we can be home by summer solstice.

Because a messenger ship is leaving from Italy tomorrow, for Alexandria, I've gathered together the recent letters I have written to Olympus and Theophilus. (Nothing for Berenice — what would I say? *Have you strangled another husband?*) Surely they will grow faint when they see the volume of my words. A princess who misses her friends has much to express. I pray there will be no storms on the great sea, or serpents.

To be stupidly honest I'm not sure who to pray to — Poseidon, Neptune, Isis, or the Unnamed God? There is Zeus, Apollo, dozens more, but I do not know which one is most likely to listen to a girl.

This morning I visited Father in his garden where his reader was reciting lines from Homer. I dismissed the servant with a wave of my hand for I wanted to be alone with my father.

He did not look well. When I asked about the soldiers, he walked away from me, over to the fountain where he began splashing his face. I stepped around to the other side so he would see me, but he remained busy washing his ears, then cleaning his teeth with his finger.

"Father, please talk to me." My voice was full of tears. When he would not answer or even look at me I burst out crying. There must be something he is not telling me.

How I wanted to scream my fury at him, my frustration. I wanted to rage, to weep.

Even so, there remained a part of me — a small part — that wanted to behave as a queen might. She must not lose herself to temper or else folly might capture her. The other part of me — the big part — wanted to be a thirteen-year-old daughter who is taken care of by a wise father. I wanted him to take us home <u>now</u> and promise to always keep me safe.

But as I looked at this man, the fallen king of Egypt, my father, I saw clearly as if in a vision, that this hope of mine was foolish. If one counts years, I was merely a child, but I knew I was the strong one. There was no time for me to weep and carry on.

"Come, Father." I took his hand and led him to a bench in the warm sunshine. I unwrapped the cotton shawl from my shoulders and dried his face with it. I thought in my heart that there were tears on his unshaven cheeks, for soon after I had pinned my shawl back on, his face was moist again.

Are these tears of regret? I wondered. *Does he see what he has become?* Though I feel pity for him, I am still cautious. In some ways a king reminds me of my leopard: He can be gentle and loving, but if threatened, he will kill.

To CONTINUE . . .

Father and I spent the afternoon at the soldiers' barracks. When I noticed a group of men near the stables, I left Father resting on a stool and myself went over. They were not drilling, they were playing a game!

Set into the ground about twenty paces apart were two iron stakes, each about one foot high. There were men behind each stake tossing the curved iron shoes that had been taken from dead horses, throwing them, trying to ring them onto the post.

I was thinking in my heart of what to say, or do, when an officer stepped forward, laughing. It was Marc Antony.

"Hail, Cleopatra! What brings you here today?"

Clearly he had been drinking because he reeked of wine. I did not want to waste time.

"Are you in command of these monkeys?" I asked. "For that is what they are, you know, playing games when there is work to be done."

"Princess," he said, spreading his arms in a shrug, "how does such a little thing like you get such a big temper?"

I held up my hand to shield my eyes from the sun.

"Marc Antony," I said, "how does such a big man like you have such a little brain?" At that I walked away from the stables.

Now it is evening. I am angry with myself for using sour words on a man I need for a friend. Even though Cicero dislikes Antony, I do not. I rather enjoy his wit and his good looks.

What is the matter with me?

Aprilis, Spring!!

Spent today in the city, at the Forum. The court was seated, as they say, lawyers for both sides had arrived and the magistrates were ready (so many clean white togas!).

From where I sat, high up in the gallery with other spectators, I could hear Cicero clearly. His speech went on for six hours, until his last water clock ran out. Because there are three water clocks per Roman hour, there were nearly twenty of these little machines on the table in front of him — such noise, all this clicking! Why can't they use an hourglass? A slave could watch and turn it when needed.

In any event, Cicero was defending a man accused of trying to strangle a shop girl; this girl then apparently cut off his ear with her own dagger. The trial was in its third day because the law allows a prosecutor six hours and the defense nine hours. An entire day was spent examining one witness. O, the lies and fakery I heard.

My heart is heavy to admit that I found Cicero's strategy unsavory. He attacked the girl's character in such embarrassing detail. O, I was shocked to hear it. This is his argument: So what if the man tried to strangle her? She must have deserved it, and now this poor fellow has only one ear.

I have learned that Roman law does not take a person's silence as an admission of guilt. Yet even though this girl did not speak a word in her defense, the court still found her guilty. Cicero won the case.

She has chosen exile over being stoned to death. Now she will live out her days on one of Italy's remote islands.

It seemed to me, by her manner and young face, that she is about fifteen years old.

I ponder the meaning of justice. As queen, will I have a heart of stone or a heart of flesh? This I do not know yet.

When I returned to the villa, Neva had my bath ready and a surprise. Letters! I had written Olympus about a cut on my wrist that had not healed. His response:

> . . . *Now then, about that sore on your arm. Prepare a poultice of figs and apply it to the wound, leave on overnight for five nights and you will recover. . . .*
>
> *I observed my first brain surgery under the skilled knife of Titus. The patient lay awake through the entire procedure, even telling memories from his boyhood. He experienced no pain, and lives to this day. . . .*

I miss Olympus! If I were in Alexandria I could observe these medical classes, too. I could be in the great Library. O, I must stop yearning so much for what I do not have, it only puts sorrow in my heart.

Rome does have a library, though a small one compared to home. Julia and I were there together when a little boy about the age of seven ran up to her. His name is

Octavian and he is the grandnephew of Julius Caesar. He looks sickly to me, quite thin and pale, but he is very sweet.

Upon introductions, Octavian took my hand and led me to a garden outside, where there was a pond with baby ducks swimming about. He had made a little boat of papyrus and sticks, so we played together, he on one side of the pond, myself on the other, pushing the boat back and forth. The ducklings merely paddled out of the way each time the boat sailed into them.

He reminds me of my brother Ptolemy, who has no cares but for his own amusements. But such is the duty of children, to play.

Theoplilus, friend and student, to Cleopatra, the princess with as many questions as there are stars in the sky:

I write in Hebrew so you will not forget all my teachings. You ask me why Isis will not answer your prayers for coming home to Alexandria. You ask me why your food offerings at the Temple of Castor and Pollux remain on the statues until mice carry them away.

O Cleopatra, do you not know? Have you not heard?

Your idols are silver and gold, stone and wood, made by the hands of men. They have mouths but cannot speak; eyes but they cannot see; they have ears but cannot hear; nor is there breath in their mouths. Those who make them will be like them, and so will all who trust in them.

No dear friend, Olympus and I have not found your beautiful leopard. I am sorry. We will keep searching for her until your return.

I MAIUS

A visitor arrived at the villa this morning early, before dawn. Marc Antony. It turns out he had not yet gone to bed!

We were so courteous to each other Neva later asked if I was feeling all right.

"Yes," I told her. "I have just decided not to be so difficult." To myself I thought, *A queen must learn how to get along with all sorts of people. I am practicing.*

We have plans for tomorrow. When Antony heard I am

eager to see the troops Father has hired, he said he personally would take me to Ostia to check the ships.

Thus my pleasant manner today reaped a pleasant result.

On another subject . . . just before bed I saw Neva and Puzo in the garden. He was holding her hand and looking at her with such adoration I smiled to myself. But suddenly my heart froze.

Across the courtyard, walking through an open corridor, was Father. I saw his face, then the flash of his gold belt as he turned the corner. He had seen them together!

O Isis, please make Father forget what he saw. For once, let him spend his night soaked in wine.

2 MAIUS

My feet are sore, my palms have blisters, but this day I am the happiest princess alive. It is quite late as I write this, all in the household of Atticus are sleeping.

I had expected Antony to pick me up in a carriage of some sort, so that Neva and I could ride together out of the weather.

But no. The clatter of hooves on the stone road was a

chariot pulled by three galloping horses! Antony stood with the reins in his hands, sturdy looking in his soldier's tunic and boots. I was ready to protest. I wanted my maid and guard to accompany me, and I certainly did not want to stand up for sixteen rough miles, then back again.

But I thought in my heart, I am a girl of thirteen and I am learning how to not always have things my own way.

I stepped up into the chariot. It was so narrow my dress brushed against Antony's sword, our arms touched.

"Hold tight, here," he said, showing me how to grasp the bronze rim. Then without another word he shook the reins and we were off, down the sandy road that ran along the Tiber, westward to the coast. I turned to look over my shoulder and saw a horseman riding fast, my good man Puzo.

I had not felt wind in my hair like this since I was at sea, in the bow of Father's ship. The air was cold on my neck and bare arms, but the sun on my face was warm. Of course, I could not hear a word of what Antony was shouting to me because of the noise, such jangling of harnesses and the rolling swish of the tall wheels in the dirt.

Soon I smelled the salt air, then I saw the sea. O, joy! The busy port of Ostia excited me for ships were coming and going, workers were on docks loading and unloading cargo. It reminded me so much of my beloved Alexandria.

Antony took me to the soldiers' barracks. (Puzo stayed an arm's length from me, his hand on the hilt of his sword at all times.) I saw men training, marching. We toured the beach where Roman galleys lay on their sides, having barnacles scraped from their hulls so they would move faster through the waves. The harbor master told me that my father's fleet had been out of the water last month, scraped, and with new tar pressed between the beams for a better seal. All was ready.

By the time Antony returned me to Rome it was sunset. I could smell aromas from the street kitchens, meat roasting and fresh onions. O, I was famished, having not eaten since breakfast. My fingers ached from holding on so tight that I could not unstrap my sandals. It took Neva an hour to untangle my windblown hair and she said my face is so burned I look wretched, like girls who toil in fields under a hot sun.

But I suffer only from the most pleasant fatigue. And from knowing we will soon be able to leave for Egypt. My heart is merry, also, because Antony and I did not quarrel. Not once during the entire day.

Summer Again

Should I complain because once again I am in a villa on the sea? Atticus has graciously sent me here, he has proven to be more a friend than I had first thought. But all is not well with him.

Cicero spoke a violent argument before the Senate, attacking Atticus' character and others who want to help us. He said the moneylenders are fools to squander good money and good soldiers on Egypt, especially under a commander like Antony who is (these are his words) "nothing more than a wretched, insignificant, intoxicated subordinate of Caesar's." I was in the gallery when Cicero also pleaded his case against my father, King Ptolemy XII.

"He is just the drunken Flute Player," he said. "It is only a matter of time before Alexandria becomes a Roman province."

Oh, I was crushed at his words, crushed. I wanted to run and hide so I could weep privately, but I stayed, for a queen must bear bad news with dignity. (I must learn to do this, I must!) Also, I did not want the ladies sitting with me to think I am merely a child. But silently my heart was screaming, *We will never let you barbarians have our beautiful city.*

Here is the sad story. Father is ready to sail home, the soldiers are ready, our ships are ready. But we must stay in Italy until the Senate hears all the legal arguments. Politics!

It is good that I am here at the sea, away from the quarrels. My admiration of Cicero has fallen — I thought he was my friend. The very words I once found enchanting have been used against me.

My comfort is the white cat, who I carried on my lap the entire journey from Rome. The curtains on my carriage stayed closed along the Appian Way, so the beautiful countryside appeared as a silky blue scene. I did not want to see the crosses in bright sunlight.

I wish Crassus would take the remaining ones down. The sight of them, though few, chills my heart. No matter how friendly we have all become, life still boils down to one ugly truth: It is folly to be an enemy of Rome.

All morning I sat on the beach looking out at the beautiful sea. I no longer feel safe knowing that powerful Roman men are quarreling about my father and our Alexandria, or that even the great Cicero will argue to his advantage. Also, I am uneasy about my father personally. If he has any thoughts on the romance between Puzo and Neva, he is keeping them to himself. I do not know if he has forgotten or if he plans to take action.

Another truth for a princess: It is folly to be an enemy of the king.

Early Morning

Little Octavian is here, such a dear child! Julia, his aunt, brought him from the sweltering heat of Rome. Already the sunshine and sea breezes have improved his complexion and he is most cheerful. But he has begged to stay with me instead of her because the villa she is living in this summer is in Pompeii, a few miles inland, much too far away for a boy anxious to build sand forts on the beach.

Thus, by staying at the villa of Atticus, Octavian can run from his room into the water whenever he pleases, and play in the waves. (We are so alike on this!)

Two days later, sunset

Some days my heart is so lonely, it feels as if I am a bird sitting alone on a roof. I watch the sea and wish my little island Antirrhodus was in the bay, near enough for me to swim to. Would sitting in my own palace make me feel more at home?

In my mind I see Marc Antony in his soldier's tunic, coming for me, his warship ready to sail for Egypt.

I think about him often.

> *Princess Cleopatra to Olympus, student of medicine, and Theophilus, student of philosophy, both friends much missed:*
>
> *Mercy to you and peace. Summer solstice passed a few weeks ago. A grain ship is now anchored in the Bay of Naples, on its way to Alexandria. I can see from my window the mariners rowing to shore in little boats to gather supplies from town. Their pilot has promised to take this letter to you so I will hurry.*
>
> *Heartache describes my daily thoughts. In fact, as I write this I am in great distress (which is why*

my words are in Greek not Hebrew, Theophilus).
Cicero says that it is against ancient Sibylline
prophecies for Romans to help Father reclaim his
throne, thus for now we must remain in Italy. (I
do not understand!)

In the meantime, the seaside villa of Atticus
comforts me.

Someone is tapping on my door. My candle is lit
to make wax for my seal. Know it is I, dear
friends, your Cleopatra, who writes this in my
own hand.

SCROLL I2
55 B.C.

ROME
WINTER AGAIN

I have not written for weeks, for I have been low in spirit.

Suffice to say that the week of Saturnalia, which started the seventeenth of December, passed with loud celebrations and feasting to honor the Roman harvest god. For seven days, courts of law and public businesses were closed. Even slaves were free to attend the festivities.

I, Princess Cleopatra, did not enjoy one moment. Each time Father tried to pull me into the crowded streets for dancing, I told him Saturn is a <u>Roman</u> god, leave me alone. Truth is, I am homesick, but he does not understand the heart of a fourteen-year-old girl.

O, yes, I am now fourteen. Dear Atticus held a small dinner in my honor a few weeks ago. It was simple and exactly to my pleasing. Two readers stood in opposite corners of the room, reciting in unison *The Birds*, a cheerful fantasy about a city in the sky, written so very long ago by Aristophanes.

It was a satisfactory evening, I must admit. Especially my unexpected meeting with Cicero. At first my heart was hard toward him, but he soon won my favor with his pleasantries. I asked him to step outside with me in the courtyard. Torches and charcoal fires placed around the fountain made the winter night feel balmy.

"Sir." I had returned to addressing Cicero formally. "It is you who stands between my father's and my returning to our home. Why?"

O, the speech that followed . . . oratory at its finest! I listened patiently, as a queen should, then I said, "Sir, you yourself know that Rome will benefit from a friendship with Egypt. The sooner my father is restored to his throne, the sooner we can work to repay the loans citizens have made." Cicero opened his mouth to speak, but I had not finished. "For it is their personal money, sir, not yours." At that, I turned and left him in the courtyard. How long he stood there I do not know, because he did not return to my party.

I am writing this while wrapped in a thick wool blanket, for my chamber feels damp. Rain is coming in through the opening above the atrium, splashing the marble floors all the way into the hall. This architecture is good for summer heat, but all this openness can be miserable in winter.

3 FEBRUARIUS

Good news. O, joy! We <u>are</u> going home, as soon as the winter storms have passed. I have already written Theophilus and Olympus, so the letters can go out on the messenger ships that will precede our royal fleet. I will be so thrilled to see them once again. This is what happened: Cicero pleaded his case before the Senate so that records show his opinion. His words:

"Marc Antony is going to Alexandria in defiance of the Senate, and of patriotism, and of the will of heaven."

Cicero then held up his hands as if symbolically washing himself of his responsibility with us, and stormed out of the building. He will not give us his blessing, but he will not keep us from leaving.

I do not know how the great Cicero will write about this event, but I hope in my heart that he remembers the many pleasant hours he and I enjoyed in conversation together.

To continue . . .

An odd thing happened today, which I am struggling to understand. Neva and I were touring some of the shops that are near the Forum. Puzo was not with us for I had decided on impulse to go out on our own.

Neva carried a basket over her arm for our purchases. We had just come out of a little book stall where I bought a volume of Catullus' poetry, when it began to rain. In moments the streets were a river of waste, so I stood on a stepping stone to keep my feet clean. My wet hair was streaming in my face, my shawl was soaked.

Suddenly I felt myself being lifted up, thrown over a man's shoulder, and carried away. When I realized this was not Puzo, for he has never carted me off in such a manner, I was frightened. I pounded my fists on the man's back. He was wearing a sword. Even though I was upside down, I managed to grab it by its handle and pull it out. But in doing so, the blade cut off his belt and sliced through the cloth of his tunic, dropping his clothes to the ground. At this, my captor set me down in the shelter of a warm bakery. I quickly stepped backward and turned to look up at his face, for I did not want to see the undressed part of his body.

It was Marc Antony. And he was laughing.

At first I was too angry to speak. Neva hurried to my side and helped brush my dress back in place and refasten my shawl, but I held onto the sword. (O, why had I thought I would be safe without Puzo?)

"Here, Commander," said a soldier stepping between us. He draped a long red cape over Antony's shoulders so he was no longer naked.

I felt my courage return. "How dare you!" I tightened my grip on the sword.

"But, Princess," he said, "are you not happier being out of the rain?" He was still smiling, obviously pleased with himself. A crowd had gathered in the wet street to watch, but the baker clapped his hands at them to leave.

"I am not happy that a brute has laid hands on me in an improper way." I pointed the sword at his face and thought how easy it would be for me to slice off his ear. I wanted to hurt him, but reason cleared my head.

I did not want to find myself in a Roman courtroom with Cicero accusing me. Nor did I want to say the wrong thing to Antony, the man I would depend on to lead soldiers to Egypt, to reclaim Father's throne. I needed to be wise.

I bent down to pick up the scabbard, slipped in the

sword, then wrapped it with the leather belt that had fallen at his feet.

"Thank you, Cleopatra," he said, reaching for it. But I backed away from him, put the sword in Neva's basket, and walked out of the bakery. It was still raining. As we turned the corner, I noticed the red cape of my commander. He was now standing in the street surrounded by other soldiers. I could see that his face was turned toward me.

It is late, the house is once again quiet. I have locked Antony's sword in my chest. It is made from beautiful Damascus steel, polished to show my reflection, but sharpened to kill. He will never know how fast my heart was beating during our encounter this afternoon. I was frightened . . . I was furious . . .

O Isis, forgive me, but now I am confused. There is something about Antony that makes me want to see him again.

13 Februarius

My spirits are higher as spring grows near. I have not seen Antony since that rainy day, but I find myself looking for him, hoping he will come to visit Atticus when I happen to be there, also.

Julia coaxed me to another play. While we were carried through the street in our litters, I saw her arm point out from her curtain, in the direction of a new theater being built. She had told me earlier it will be the first one made of stone and will be named the Theater of Pompey, after her husband.

TWO DAYS LATER

I am still pale from my afternoon at the theater and will try to record the events that so upset me.

Julia and I were in the front row as usual, enjoying the satire, *The Frogs*. Suddenly a man sitting far behind me shouted, "O, shut up!" apparently to one of the actors. As a royal princess I did not turn around to see who this brute was, but I could see that people alongside me were restless. To my surprise, someone else yelled, "Shut up, you pig!" then others joined in. I tried to keep my eyes on the performers, but they, too, were distracted.

Voices rose from the audience, calling for something more interesting, a bear eating a man perhaps or gladiators killing one another. I glanced at Julia. She stared straight ahead, but her mouth moved in a slight grimace, the only hint that she was as displeased as I.

Then before our eyes, with actors still on stage, a lioness was brought out, its legs hobbled together so she would not leap into the stands. She looked starved, and I wondered if she was the one brought from Alexandria with our fleet so many months ago. When a slave was then dragged out, the crowd began chanting.

"Crucify him!"

My hands twisted nervously in my lap, hidden by the folds of my toga. Meanwhile the actors carried on with the play, trying to shout above the noise.

O Isis, I will not describe the slave's terrible cries when the lion's front paws were unchained. Because I was in the front row, those sitting behind me could not see that my royal eyes were closed. Tears were in my throat. I did not want to see such cruelties.

When a gladiator came out to finish off the lion, the audience went wild. My heart wanted to weep for I now knew another ugly truth: Men prefer brutality to literature. I suffered sitting there, not knowing what to do. When prisoners were led to the dirt area in front of the stage, carrying beams of wood across their shoulders, I looked for Puzo.

I saw him moving off to the side, near an exit, so I patted Julia's arm. We both stood and walked out. I, Cleopatra, Princess of the Nile, do not have to watch crucifixions.

May Rome burn. I want to go home.

8 Martius
Aboard the royal ship Roga

It is cold on deck as I write. Wind pushes at our sails so that we are tilted almost onto our side, but I am not afraid. We have just weighed anchor out from the island of Malta and are heading south. Within one week we should be home.

My heart is cheered by many things.

Father is alert and dressed like a king. I have not seen him drunk since our last party in Rome. What a scene that was!

Our fleet and the Roman warships are spread out over miles of the great sea. Foot soldiers led by Marc Antony left many weeks ago to march into Alexandria by way of Judea. They should arrive at the same time we do.

Why can I not stop thinking of him?

The farewell banquet for Antony hosted by Atticus was lavish. I was so busy in my thoughts about our departure to take place the following day that my memory is vague over who and how many dignitaries took my hand in greeting. The rooms were loud with voices and the music of harps and tambourines. In every corner there were little balls of incense to mask the foul odors of vomit, for there was much drinking of wine — too much.

Many times that evening, I excused myself to the kitchen garden where the air was cool. It was here that I was surprised by Antony waiting for me by the gate. It was odd that I could find no words to speak, nor did he. We just stood there near the rows of newly planted herbs and looked around as if we were two shoppers in the marketplace. There was no moonlight at this hour, just a low glow of candles along the path leading into the next courtyard. Thus when he pulled me into his arms I could not see his face. I did not know what to do, but I was not as alarmed as when he had hoisted me over his shoulder.

He kissed me.

Was it the heavy smell of wine on his breath that made me back away, or was I just nervous? Perhaps both.

Now that our ships are in full sail I wonder when we will reach Alexandria and, when we do, if Antony and I will find another moment to be alone.

Neva has just passed a note to me. This morning Father

caught her and Puzo in a tender embrace. She is terrified that he will sentence her to the ocean serpents. I must hurry to prevent this.

II Martius

My worry for Puzo and Neva was saved when a storm hit for Father was distracted and nervous. He lashed himself to the mast, the safest place for a king, then when the skies cleared he was again distracted because there came much shouting for joy.

Alexandria!

I am too excited for words. We are home.

16 Martius
The Royal Palace of Alexandria

Will I give away the secrets of my heart if I describe how it was to finally see Olympus again? I had not realized how deep my affection is for him, this friend of my youth. Thoughts of Marc Antony moved far back in my mind.

After two years, Olympus was taller and, now sixteen, his chest as broad as a man's. I could see him standing on the palace steps that lead down into the water. Our ship was anchored further out so a little boat took me to him. I was so anxious though, I jumped in before we landed and found myself in the swells up to my waist. I reached for his outstretched hand.

When Olympus embraced me, I wept with relief. *O, my friend, I have missed you.* There were so many things I wanted to tell him. Theophilus was there, too, more reserved, but he did give me a warm handshake. Meanwhile the harbor was spilling over with Roman soldiers and horses. I wondered what "Queen" Berenice was doing at this moment.

To continue . . .

I found Her Royal Highness in the bath. She seemed surprised and delighted to see me, but I thought in my heart she must be out of her mind. Could she not hear the crowds in the streets and the horses running, the shouts and clashing of swords?

I refused the goblet of wine her servant brought to me. For months I had practiced what I would say to my sister when this moment arrived.

"Father wants to see you."

30 Aprilis

O, it was a sorrowful Berenice who wept at Father's feet. He sat on his throne, once more Pharaoh, Ptolemy XII, the mighty King of Egypt. He looked at her bowed figure and waved to a guard, who removed the royal purple cloak from her back. He waved again, and my sister was led out of the room.

I stood quietly at his side. He smiled up at me, then struck his scepter three times against the floor. An official brought the purple cloak to me and ceremoniously draped it over my shoulders. I bowed to Father and backed out of the room.

Evening

I write from my chamber. Pharos Lighthouse glows above the waves of my home shore. So many months away, I should be more joyful to be here. But something happened today that has made my heart quiet.

I wanted to be bold with Father about my two servants. Neva and Puzo love each other, I planned to tell him. I want a royal edict that says they may marry and continue to serve in the palace. The speech was in my mind for days, a persuasive line of reasoning I had learned from Cicero. Father would not refuse me, I knew it.

When I appeared before him there was quite a lot of activity. Dancers off to one side, musicians on the other, soldiers standing around. Marc Antony passed me in the corridor on his way out. He dipped his head in greeting, but said nothing. I wanted to talk to him, about anything or nothing, but this obviously was not the time.

When Father saw me, he opened his arms wide and smiled. "O Cleopatra," he said. "You grow more lovely by the hour. What is it you desire, my daughter?"

I stood near a thick marble column and took a breath. But before my words began, I heard soldiers marching down a hall toward us. Father looked up at the Roman leading the procession and beckoned him to step forward. I turned to look, but was not prepared for the sight awaiting me.

Had I been just a girl, I would have fainted. Even so, I placed my hand against the column to steady myself.

Blood spilled onto the mosaic floor from a bronze shield that was being carried as a tray. On this tray was the severed head of my sister, Berenice.

I MAIUS

I am still pondering in my heart the events of yesterday, feeling sadness for the terror Berenice must have felt when she realized her fate. Father gave her the ultimate punishment. He showed no mercy at all.

Now I am next in line to the throne.

A heaviness weighs on me now that I have seen what Father does to a daughter who displeases him. If he gets angry with me or thinks I am disloyal or wants to make sure I do not become queen, will he order my execution, too? Will my little brothers and Arsinoë try to kill me so one of them may be pharaoh?

Great sorrow overwhelms me this day. I had thought that once we were home again, away from Roman territory, I would be safe.

10 MAIUS

Olympus and I met in the Library. Soon Theophilus joined us, a thick scroll under his arm. We were once more old friends, ready to study and talk. It was as if we had not lost one day together. They wanted to know everything about Rome, but they were most curious about Marc Antony and boldly asked if I have affection for this barbarian.

I did not know how to answer. What would they say if I told them about the kiss in the garden? How can I explain to them my heart when there is also sadness and worry?

"Cleopatra," said Olympus, "when you left for Rome you were just a girl of twelve. Now you are a young woman, capable of much responsibility. We can see that you are wiser in the ways of the world, especially the Roman world."

"Yes," I said.

Theophilus looked up from the scroll he had been reading. He said, "Your older sisters are dead, your father is weak. If he meets an untimely death, you may be pharaoh. Are you ready, Cleopatra? Would you have allies in Rome?"

I stood and went out to the courtyard. My friends did not follow because they knew I needed to think.

What they say is true. Because of my father, Rome and Alexandria are now linked with each other. For Egypt to survive I need allies, it is my royal duty to cultivate powerful friends. There is also an unspoken word for ally: "husband."

Caesar is strong, but I do not know him. Crassus is just a politician, too greedy to trust. Pompey is crude and so impressed with himself, he would not make a loyal friend. Cicero might be worthy and would certainly win opinions in the Senate, but he does not command an army. Then there is Marc Antony, a leader of men and with a definite charm, I must admit.

Of all the barbarians, I am most interested in Antony.

13 MAIUS

Last night I was awaked by an unusual sound: soft footsteps.

I lay in bed trying to listen, my heart pounding. *Who was there?* When I realized that neither Puzo or Neva had stirred, terror seized my heart. Had they been murdered in their sleep and now their killer was coming after me?

Slowly I moved my hand down the side of my bed where my dagger is hidden. A shadow low to the ground was crawling toward me. I held my breath, wanting to hear the precise moment when I should stab my attacker.

But the sound I heard was purring.

"Arrow?" I whispered.

She came to me like an old friend, rubbing her large head against my arm. She licked my hand and rolled onto her side. O, was I happy to see her. I hugged her tight while she kneaded her claws in my blanket, purring and telling me all about it, but where she hid all these months, I will never know. I thank the gods that Tryphaena had not hunted her down and killed her.

TO CONTINUE . . .

I do not want to write about the bloodshed in Alexandria, but will say that Berenice was not the only one who lost her head. Now soldiers are camped outside the city walls and along the beaches, our harbors are crowded with their anchored ships. As Marc Antony is their commander he is busy with military duties. He and I have not seen each other since the day of my sister's execution.

Bucephalus was safe in the royal stables. O, she was a beautiful sight! Our reunion was brief, though, because of danger in the streets. We will have to wait until things quiet down before taking our favorite rides. Meanwhile I must carry on with my studies. There is so much to learn and prepare for if ever I am to become queen.

A dispatch from Antony arrived yesterday. It was written by one of his secretaries because he injured his hand in a fight. Troops will be leaving Egypt soon, some by sea, but many will march east back into Judea, another Roman province. Antony said it could take one year for him to go around the edge of the continent back to Italy, but I think he wants to take his time, perhaps delaying an encounter with Cicero.

Word also reached us that Julius Caesar is planning to invade and conquer Brittania this summer. He has eighty warships ready to cross the channel from Gaul.

I have written letters to these men — Antony, Cicero, and Caesar — letters of friendship with invitations. I will welcome seeing them under peaceful circumstances. I wanted to say more to Antony, but did not know how or even what those thoughts would be.

THE NEXT DAY

I visited the little ones in the nursery. Arsinoë is more beautiful than I remember, and at eleven years clearly rules our brothers. Ptolemy is six and Ptolemy the Younger is four, still babies. For now, they are no threat to Father or myself.

I have been pondering the sorrows of my heart and have made a decision.

If I am to be queen I must learn more about the Egyptian people but I can not accomplish this by sitting around the palace. Thus, in ten days I will set sail aboard the royal barge for a trip up the Nile. I want to see the Great Pyramids, the Sphinx, and all the villages along the way. With me will be the usual guards, cooks, and servants. Puzo and Neva of course, and Arrow (who follows me everywhere now).

Olympus has been granted leave from medical school for the purpose of studying native diseases and remedies. My heart soars knowing he will be my companion. Our friend Theophilus will remain in Alexandria as he is training to become a rabbi. I know he will be a fine one.

When I met with Father in the throne room, I did not tell him the whole story. If he knew my trip was planned for the purpose of making me a good queen, that I am seeking wisdom and knowledge, he might prefer to kill me. Thus, he has given his blessing. He believes this adventure is merely the frolic of a fourteen-year-old girl, yet he also said he is planning my wedding, which will take place upon my return.

It grieves me that I still fear my own father, and that I must marry the man he chooses. But such is the destiny of a daughter in the Royal House of Ptolemy.

Who this husband will be, I do not know.

12 Junius
Aboard the royal barge Isis

The heat of my Egypt burns down on us all day. But there is shade under our canopy and a slight breeze off the water. Rowers strain against the river's strong current, sometimes helped along when a favorable wind catches our sail. I am pleased to be once again on a voyage, seeing new things. But this time, I am not frightened of what lies ahead or worried how others will receive me.

Olympus has arranged a desk up here by the mast, which is where I now sit. He does not bother me when I am writing, nor I him, for he is keeping a medical journal; we take turns rotating the hourglass. I look up to see the banks of the Nile slip by. Flocks of herons and flamingos fly up from the marshes, making streaks of blue, pink, and white in the sky. The sounds of frogs and birds and water lapping against our hull is music to me, beautiful music.

There are clusters of mud huts in each village, Egyptian children always playing near the shore. It seems they know where crocodiles hide and are able to keep away from them.

My heart is at peace. The only worry for those who travel this broad green river is drowning, often caused by the hippopotamus. These creatures love to hide in the water until a boat comes along, then ram it until the occupants fall overboard. I have seen this happen. But when my guards tried to kill one by beating it over the head with an oar I stopped them, for Egyptians believe the hippo is goddess of childbirth.

Compared to the Roman arena, the Nile is as safe as heaven.

Late Afternoon

We are about to dock at a village called Po-sep. Donkeys are walking in a circle, pulling buckets of water up from the river by a crude wheel. Children have crowded the bank and already are pointing to our beautiful flags and pennants.

Did I mention that during our last stop I had an Egyptian priest at the Temple of Isis marry my dear Puzo and Neva? At least on our trip, which may take two years, they can have the joy of being married. There are plenty of days ahead, for me to think of ways to present this to Father.

Time to put my writing tools in my little chest. Local officials and my cooks are preparing a banquet among a grove of date palms. O, its shade is inviting. I see a child waving to me; another is throwing sweetly scented flowers onto the water.

"Princess," they are calling. "Welcome . . . we welcome you."

Epilogue

Following Egyptian custom, Cleopatra married her brother, Ptolemy XIII, and upon their father's death in 51 B.C. they became corulers. She was eighteen, he was ten.

Approximately three years earlier, Julia, the beloved daughter of Caesar, died in childbirth, leaving him heartbroken and her husband, Pompey, devastated. Her untimely death, however, loosened the political ties between these two leaders, and they stopped pretending to be friends. Pompey realized he was the last obstacle in Caesar's rise to power, so he fled with his family to Egypt, hoping to gain asylum with Cleopatra and her brother because at one time they had been under his guardianship.

It was an unfortunate miscalculation. He didn't realize the thirteen-year-old Ptolemy wanted to gain favor with Rome and was not in the least concerned with old friendships. One of Ptolemy's advisers suggested murdering Pompey because, after all, "Dead men don't bite." Thus when Pompey sailed into Alexandria's harbor in the fall of 48 B.C and stepped ashore, he was swiftly beheaded, supposedly as his children and screaming wife watched from their boat. When some days later Julius Caesar arrived in Egypt as conqueror, Ptolemy presented him with a royal gift: the severed, pickled head of Pompey the Great, along with his ring. It is said that Caesar wept at the loss of his former friend and son-in-law.

Meanwhile Cleopatra, age twenty-one, went into hiding and devised a more ingenious way to meet the famous Roman, who was about fifty-two years old at the time. She rolled herself up in a rug and had her servant carry her into Caesar's private quarters. He was smitten with her. They became lovers, and in June 47 B.C. a son was born to them, Ptolemy XV Caesarion.

In 44 B.C., Caesar was assassinated in Rome by a group of senators. He was succeeded by his legal heir, seventeen-year-old Octavian. One year later, another assassination took place: Marc Antony was so angry about the critical things Cicero had written and said about him in the Senate that he ordered Cicero's head and right hand cut off. These grisly items he displayed at the speaker's platform in Rome. It is said that Antony's wife at the time, Fulvia, took one of her hairpins and pierced Cicero's tongue with it.

A few years after Caesar's death, Cleopatra and Marc Antony fell in love and, according to some historians, were married in an Egyptian ceremony. They had three children: twins Alexander Helios and Cleopatra Selene, and Ptolemy Philadelphus. Together they tried to protect the city of Alexandria, for Octavian had declared war against the Egyptian queen.

In September of 31 B.C., Antony and Cleopatra chose to fight a crucial battle at sea, but their fleet was crushed. Months later, Octavian and his army swept into Alexandria. Realizing that Egypt would be conquered, Cleopatra arranged for her fourteen-year-old son, Caesarion, to escape because she wanted to ensure that the Ptolemaic line would continue. He fled to India with a large sum of money but was murdered before he reached safety.

Humiliated by the military defeat and mistakenly thinking that Cleopatra was dead, Antony stabbed himself with his sword. As he bled to death from his wounds, friends carried him to the queen's hiding place, where he died in her arms. Later she, too, took her life, apparently by allowing a deadly snake to bite her.

Cleopatra and her physician, Olympus, remained close personal friends her entire life.

After Cleopatra's death, her children by Marc

Antony — Alexander and Cleopatra, now ten years old, and Ptolemy, age six — were sent to Italy to be cared for by Antony's Roman fourth wife, Octavia. The boys later disappeared under mysterious circumstances. Their sister survived to marry King Juba II of Mauretania, and they had two children, Ptolemy and Drusilla.

Some accounts show that Drusilla married Marcus Antonius Felix, the Roman governor of Judea. While in court she and Felix listened to testimony by the Apostle Paul, who was on trial for his belief in Jesus Christ (Acts 24:24).

HISTORICAL NOTE

Cleopatra VII was born in 69 B.C. and she died in 30 B.C., but little is known about her early years.

What information has survived through the centuries often is contradictory and confusing, as is the repetitive use of royal names and the variety of spellings. As a result, researchers often come to different conclusions. For example, what did Cleopatra look like? Some think that Egyptian blood may have given her dark hair and brown eyes; others suggest her Macedonian ancestry made her light-skinned, possibly with blonde hair and green eyes. There is also the question of Cleopatra's age when she met Marc Antony. Some experts say she was a young princess; others insist she was already queen and in her late twenties.

With respect to other historical figures and events portrayed in this story, every attempt has been made to be as accurate as possible.

It has been said that Alexandria's great library was destroyed in 48 B.C. during a civil war, after Julius Caesar had conquered the city. To protect the harbor from Egyptian soldiers and to keep them from seizing all the warships anchored there, Caesar set torches to the fleet. Unfortunately, the roaring flames spread from the docks to the warehouses to the library. It is unknown how many scrolls and manuscripts were lost in this fire.

But we do have the later writings of Plutarch, one of the great biographers of antiquity. He was born in Greece about A.D. 46 and traveled to Rome and Alexandria, possibly hearing first- or secondhand from those who'd known Cleopatra. He wrote:

> Their acquaintance was with her when a girl, young and ignorant of the world.
>
> ... Her actual beauty, it is said, was not in itself so remarkable that none could be compared with her, or that no one could see her without being struck by it, but the contact of her presence, if you lived with her, was irresistible. ...
>
> It was a pleasure merely to hear the sound of her voice, with which, like an instrument of many strings, she could pass from one language to another; so that there were few of the

barbarian nations that she answered by an interpreter; to most of them she spoke herself, as to the Ethiopians, Troglodytes, Hebrews, Arabians, Syrians, Medes, Parthians, and many others, whose language she had learnt; which was all the more surprising, because most of the kings [who were] her predecessors scarcely gave themselves the trouble to acquire the Egyptian tongue, and several of them quite abandoned the Macedonian.

Plutarch's comments reveal that Cleopatra was literate and interested in people. It is quite plausible that she herself, rather than a scribe, may have recorded her thoughts and observations.

During Cleopatra's lifetime, writers used clay tablets as well as leather parchment and papyrus to record information. These papers could be glued together side by side to form one long piece, sometimes up to thirty feet wide, which would then be rolled onto a scroll simultaneously from both ends. Archaeologists have discovered manuscripts such as these that had been stored in clay jars centuries before.

Perhaps the most celebrated discovery was in 1947,

when a young Bedouin shepherd wandered into a cave near the Dead Sea in Jordan. There, he found broken jars with leather scrolls written in Aramaic and Hebrew, Biblical manuscripts dating from more than one thousand years earlier than any previously found. These documents and others from nearby caves are thought to have been a hidden library used sometime between 100 B.C. and A.D. 100 by a Jewish sect.

Scholars agree that more stories from the ancient world have yet to be found. Is it possible that a diary truly written by Cleopatra lies hidden in a cave somewhere?

A few interesting events that preceded and followed the life of Cleopatra are worth noting:

- The kingdom of ancient Egypt began before recorded history, approximately five thousand years ago, along the fertile Nile River. It lasted longer than any other civilization in the world, ruled by kings who were also thought to be living gods. Because these rulers believed their lives would continue after death they built pyramids for their tombs, to preserve the body and their earthly treasures for all eternity. Considered to be the oldest man-made monuments on earth, these pyramids were engineered and constructed so superbly that dozens are still standing. Perhaps one of the most remarkable of these is the Great Pyramid, built by Pharaoh Khufu during the 2600s B.C., near what is now the city of Cairo. As the largest tomb ever built, its base is big enough to hold eight football fields, and it is as tall as a forty-foot skyscraper.

- In 332 B.C. Alexander the Great conquered Egypt, adding it to his vast empire. After his death one of his generals, Ptolemy I, established himself as King of Egypt, which began the ptolemaic dynasty of rulers. This ended when Cleopatra died in 30 B.C., and the country was taken over by the Roman Empire.

- Four hundred years before Cleopatra was born, Spartan soldiers were using sulfur, pitch, and charcoal as "chemical warfare." Approximately two hundred years later, the Great Wall of China was completed during the Ch'in Dynasty. At the time of Cleopatra's death in 30 B.C. the magnificent Pantheon was being built in Rome and wouldn't be finished for another 150 years. Much of the city of Rome was destroyed by fire in A.D. 64. Emperor Nero blamed Christians for starting the fires and ordered scores of them to be killed, some say by having them thrown into an arena with lions.

- As a young girl Cleopatra may have vacationed in Pompeii and Herculaneum, but one hundred years after her death these lovely seaside towns had been buried under the boiling lava of Mt. Vesuvius. At least 16,000 people died when this volcano erupted in August of A.D. 79.

- After Cleopatra's suicide, Octavian appointed himself Egypt's new pharaoh and, as Rome's first emperor, he renamed himself Caesar Augustus. Some thirty years later he became linked with the birth of Jesus Christ as recorded in the Bible. "In those days Caesar Augustus issued a decree that a census should be taken of the entire Roman world" (Luke 1:2).

- Although Cleopatra died young, at age thirty-nine, she is remembered as one of the most influential women in history because of her alliances with Julius Caesar and Marc Antony. Her death marked the beginning of Roman rule in Egypt, which was to last another several hundred years.

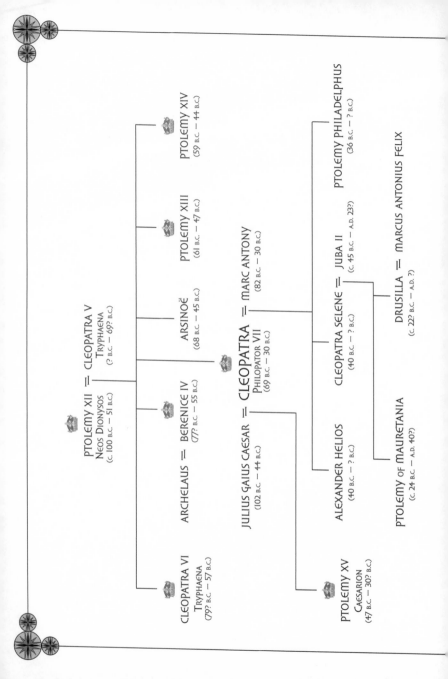

THE PTOLEMY FAMILY TREE

Alexander the Great (356 B.C. – 323 B.C.), King of Macedonia, Greece, was a brilliant military leader. He conquered many lands, including Egypt, where he established himself as king and founded the capital city of Alexandria. After Alexander died, one of his generals, Ptolemy I Soter, also a Macedonian Greek, became ruler of Egypt in 305 B.C. And so began the dynasty of the Ptolemies from which Cleopatra VII descended. The family tree chart follows the growth of the Ptolemy dynasty, beginning with the twelfth King Ptolemy, Neos Dionysos Auletes, Cleopatra's father. The same names are used throughout generations, and dates of births and deaths are not always available. The crown symbol indicates those who ruled over Egypt. Double lines represent marriages or partnerships; single lines indicate parentage.

PTOLEMY XII NEOS DIONYSOS   c. 100? B.C. – 51 B.C.
Called Auletes, or the Flute Player, Ptolemy XII ruled Egypt from 80 B.C. until his death in 51 B.C.

CLEOPATRA TRYPHAENA V   ? B.C. – 69? B.C.
Wife of Ptolemy XII

CHILDREN OF PTOLEMY XII
AND CLEOPATRA V

CLEOPATRA TRYPHAENA VI   79? B.C. – 57 B.C.

Eldest daughter of Ptolemy XII. In her father's absence,
Tryphaena seized the throne and ruled Egypt from 58 B.C.
to 57 B.C., when she was killed by her father's supporters.

BERENICE IV   77? B.C. – 55 B.C.

The second daughter of Ptolemy XII, Berenice took control
of Egypt after Tryphaena VI's death and ruled from 57 B.C.
to 55 B.C., when her father ordered her execution.

CLEOPATRA PHILOPATOR VII   69 B.C. – 30 B.C.

Third daughter of Ptolemy XII, in 51 B.C., Cleopatra
Philopator VII became Queen of Egypt at age eighteen.
She committed suicide after a twenty-one-year rule.

ARSINOË   68 B.C. – 45 B.C.

Youngest daughter of Ptolemy XII. After Cleopatra became
queen, she had Arsinoë imprisoned and sent to Rome, where
she was paraded through the streets in chains. Cleopatra
secured her throne by having Arsinoë murdered.

PTOLEMY XIII   61 B.C. – 47 B.C.

First son of Ptolemy XII. Following Ptolemaic dynastic law,
Cleopatra and Ptolemy XIII married and were joint rulers.
As a young teenager, he ordered the execution of Pompey

the Great. Months later, during a battle against Caesar, he drowned in the Nile from the weight of his golden breastplate.

PTOLEMY XIV   59 B.C. – 44 B.C.

Youngest son of Ptolemy XII. Cleopatra married him upon the death of their brother (above). He died suddenly, which freed Cleopatra to rule jointly with her three-year-old son by Caesar, Ptolemy XV Caesar, called Caesarion ("Little Caesar").

CLEOPATRA'S LOVES

JULIUS GAIUS CAESAR   102 B.C. – 44 B.C.

Roman statesman and general considered one of the greatest men in history. He ruled Rome from 49 B.C. to 44 B.C. When he and Cleopatra first met, she was twenty-one years old; he was in his early fifties. Their son was born nine months later, by some records on June 23, 47 B.C.

MARC ANTONY   82 B.C. – 30 B.C.

Born in Alexandria, Egypt, to a noble family, he was a soldier and friend of Julius Caesar, serving under him in Gaul. Together with Octavian and Marcus Aemilius Lepidus, Antony formed the Second Triumvirate. He had three children by Cleopatra and several by other wives.

CLEOPATRA'S CHILDREN

PTOLEMY XV CAESARION   47 B.C. – 30? B.C.
Oldest son of Cleopatra VII, Caesarion ("Little Caesar")
became co-ruler of Egypt with his mother after Ptolemy
XIV died. His father was Julius Caesar.

ALEXANDER HELIOS AND CLEOPATRA SELENE   40 B.C. – ?
Twin son and daughter of Cleopatra and Marc Antony. They
were named after the Greek gods of the sun and the moon.
Cleopatra Selene later became Queen of Mauretania.

PTOLEMY PHILADELPHUS   36 B.C. – ?
Youngest son of Cleopatra and Marc Antony

OTHER ROYALS IN THE PTOLEMY FAMILY

ARCHELAUS
Husband of Berenice IV

JUBA II   c.45 B.C. – A.D. 23?
King of Mauretania and husband of Cleopatra Selene

PTOLEMY OF MAURETANIA   c.24 B.C. – A.D. 40?
Firstborn of Cleopatra Selene and Juba II

DRUSILLA   c.22? B.C. – A.D. ?
  Daughter of Cleopatra Selene and Juba II

MARCUS ANTONIUS FELIX
  Roman governor of Judea and husband of Drusilla

HISTORICAL CHARACTERS AND PLACES NOT INCLUDED IN FAMILY TREE

ALEXANDER THE GREAT: [356 B.C. – 323 B.C.] King of
  Macedonia; military leader whose conquests help spread
  Greek culture throughout Egypt, India, and Asia Minor.

ALEXANDRIA: Seaport in northern Egypt at the west end of the
  Nile Delta, on the Mediterranean Sea. Founded by
  Alexander the Great.

ARISTOPHANES: [448? B.C. – 380? B.C.] Greek writer of satiric
  comedies. His plays were performed in Roman and Greek
  theaters.

AUGUSTUS, GAIUS JULIUS CAESAR OCTAVIANUS: [63 B.C. –
  A.D. 14] Legal heir to and great-nephew of Julius Caesar.
  First Roman emperor (27 B.C.– A.D. 14).

CATULLUS, GAIUS VALERIUS: [c. 84 B.C. – 54 B.C.] Roman lyrical poet

CICERO: [106 B.C. – 43 B.C.] A lawyer and one of the greatest orators of all time. His eloquent speeches are considered to be the best of ancient Roman literature. After Caesar's death, Cicero briefly led the Senate, but he was assassinated the following year on orders from Marc Antony (see Epilogue).

CRASSUS, MARCUS LICINIUS: [115? B.C. – 53 B.C.] A noted general and Roman statesman, he formed the First Triumvirate with Pompey and Caesar in 60 B.C. He crushed the revolt of Spartacus in 71 B.C.

GABINIUS, AULUS: [? B.C. – 48 B.C.] A prominent Roman who became governor of Syria. He backed Marc Antony's mission to reclaim the Egyptian throne for King Ptolemy XII.

HERCULANEUM: A Roman seaside town on the Bay of Naples destroyed by the eruption of Mt. Vesuvius in A.D. 79 along with its neighboring town, Pompeii. Herculaneum lay buried under volcanic ash for centuries until a well-digger discovered some ruins in 1709.

JULIA: [? B.C. – 54 B.C.] Daughter of Julius Caesar; married Pompey the Great. The marriage helped make an alliance between these two men, but their friendship ended when Julia died a few years later.

OCTAVIAN: See Augustus.

OLYMPUS: Cleopatra's lifelong friend and personal physician

OSTIA: Seaport on western coast of Italy, sixteen miles from Rome
via the Tiber River

PLUTARCH: [A.D. 46?– A.D. 120?] Greek biographer and historian.
He wrote about Caesar, Cleopatra, and Marc Antony.

POMPEII: See Herculaneum.

POMPEY THE GREAT: [106 B.C. – 48 B.C.] Powerful Roman
statesman and general; part of the First Triumvirate with
Caesar and Crassus. He was beheaded in Egypt
(see Epilogue).

SAPPHO: [c. 612 B.C. – 580 B.C.] Greek lyric poet

SOCRATES: [c. 469 B.C. – 399 B.C.] Greek philosopher and teacher

SPARTACUS: [? B.C. – 71 B.C.] A Thracian soldier captured by the
Romans and sold into slavery. He became a famous
gladiator. He escaped and started a slave revolt, hoping to
return to his homeland, but was defeated by Crassus's
army. Spartacus fought courageously until his death, but
the Romans, as a warning to others, crucified thousands of
his fellow slaves.

The many faces of Cleopatra… Above, a modern engraving (undated) of the young queen

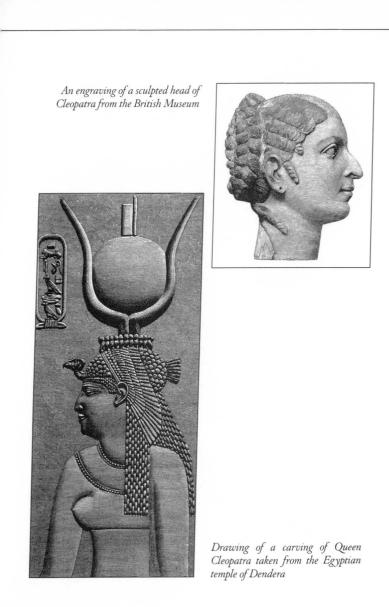

An engraving of a sculpted head of Cleopatra from the British Museum

Drawing of a carving of Queen Cleopatra taken from the Egyptian temple of Dendera

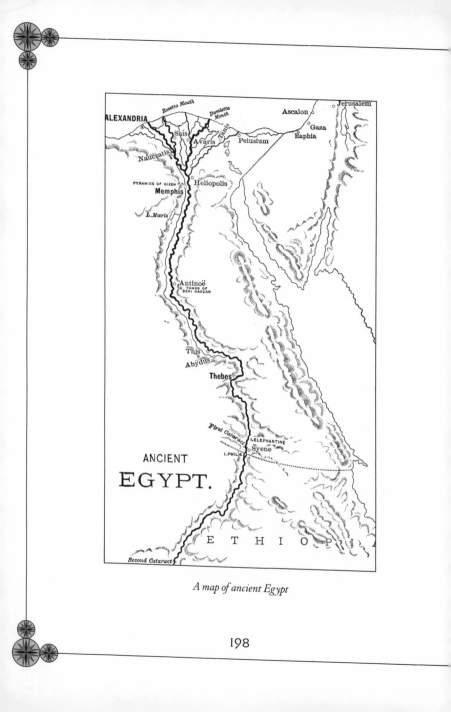

A map of ancient Egypt

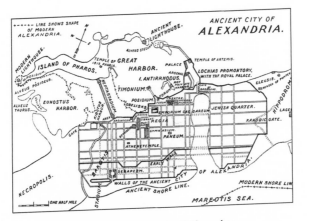

A map of the ancient city of Alexandria

A map of the vast ancient Roman Empire

PTOLEMAEVS SOTER.

Apud Fuluium Vrsinum
in nomismate argenteo.

An engraving of Ptolemy I Soter, the first Ptolemy ruler of Egypt

An engraving of King Ptolemy XII, Neos Dionysos Auletes, Cleopatra's father

Julius Caesar, from a bust in the Museum of the Louvre

Drawing of a bust of Marc Antony

An engraving of a famous statue of Augustus Caesar called the Augustus Prima Porta

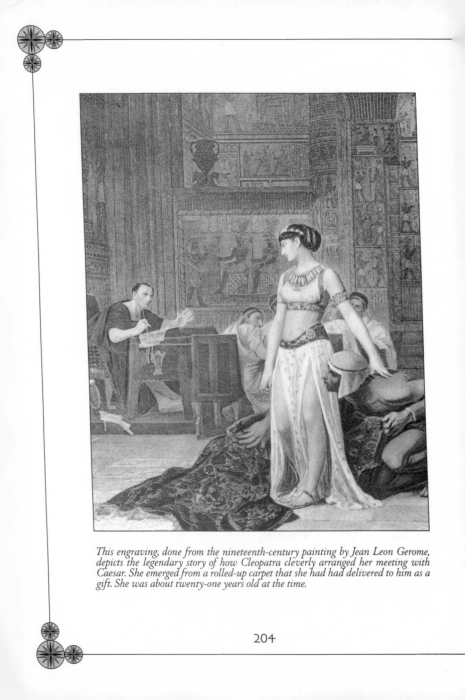

This engraving, done from the nineteenth-century painting by Jean Leon Gerome, depicts the legendary story of how Cleopatra cleverly arranged her meeting with Caesar. She emerged from a rolled-up carpet that she had had delivered to him as a gift. She was about twenty-one years old at the time.

This drawing by R. C. Woodville portrays Marc Antony being received by Queen Cleopatra and her brother, King Ptolemy XIII, at their court.

Cleopatra's barge, from a painting by H. Picou. The painter depicts a very festive atmosphere on board the queen's royal vessel.

This woodcut dramatizes the fierce sea battle at Actium, Greece, in 31 B.C. Here Octavian defeated Antony and Cleopatra, who — according to Octavian and his allies — wanted to become sole rulers of Rome. This event marked the beginning of the end for Antony and Cleopatra.

Augustus Caesar stands triumphant over the dead body of Cleopatra in this wood engraving from the title page of a nineteenth-century edition of Shakespeare's play Antony and Cleopatra.

Of the pyramids of Egypt, the Great Pyramid of Giza (foreground) is one of the Seven Wonders of the Ancient World. Twenty years in the making, the pyramid was completed about 2560 B.C. It was built as a burial tomb for Pharaoh Khufu (in Greek, Cheops). It lasted through the time of Cleopatra's rule and still stands in Giza, Egypt, today.

Near the Great Pyramid stands the famous Sphinx, an enormous sandstone statue of a pharaoh's head on a lion's body. Built more than 4,500 years ago, the monument has suffered much damage from harsh weather conditions.

Around 290 B.C., more than 200 years before Cleopatra was born, King Ptolemy I began plans to build the Lighthouse of Alexandria. It was actually built by his son Ptolemy II Philadelphos. The monument, also called Pharos Lighthouse, measured over 400 feet (equal to a forty-story skyscraper). Another of the Seven Wonders of the Ancient World, it stood for 1,500 years and was destroyed after centuries of earthquake damage.

A drawing of the interior of the Alexandrian Great Library as it may have looked during the reign of the Ptolemies

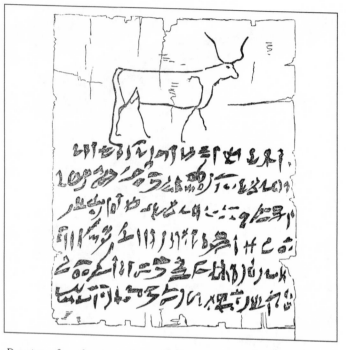

Drawing of a fragment of an Egyptian papyrus scroll that illustrates hieroglyphics. This ancient Egyptian system of writing with symbols was developed about 4000 B.C.

In hieroglyphics the line is read from right to left. Translated, this line reads, "Raising/statue/of king of Egypt/Ptolemy eternal beloved of Ptah."

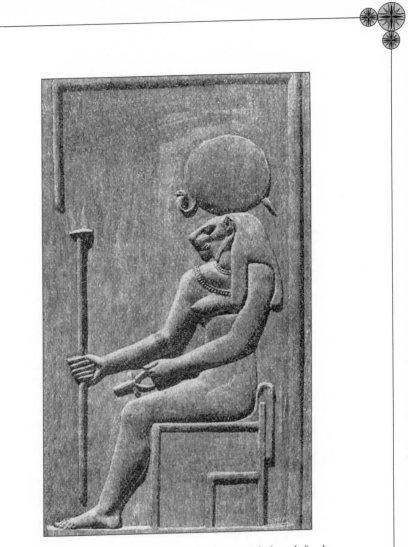

Ancient Egyptians worshipped many gods. This engraving of a bas-relief sculpture from the Cairo Museum is one representation of the goddess Isis.

Women in the Egyptian royal court wore elaborate and beautiful headdresses such as this one.

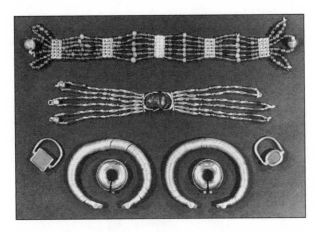

Ancient Egyptian bangles, earrings, and bracelets c. 2000 B.C. – c. A.D. 300. Jewelry was an essential part of Egyptian dressing.

Artifacts from the time period show the brilliance and ingenuity of the people. This museum piece, a game board carved from ivory, comes from the twelfth dynasty. Pieces like these are the ancestors of the modern chessboard.

About the Author

While writing *Cleopatra: Daughter of the Nile*, Kristiana Gregory was thrilled to be transported to the ancient world. "As a kid studying world history in fifth grade, my image of Cleopatra was that she wore beautiful clothes and jewels and probably spent her days floating down the river on a fancy boat. I had no idea that she was so intelligent and could speak several languages."

Gregory hopes that readers will enjoy picturing Cleopatra as a young teenager and imagining what she may have thought and felt about the world around her. "She lived during such a pivotal period of history, when the Roman Empire was the most powerful one on earth. It's exciting to imagine how Cleopatra might have responded to all this.

"Most of all, I hope that children will have as much fun reading this story as I did writing it, and that they will be encouraged to read more and more and more, about anything and everything!"

Kristiana Gregory has written numerous books for middle-grade readers, including *Orphan Runaways, Jimmy Spoon and the Pony Express, The Stowaway,* and three titles in the Dear America series: *The Winter of Red Snow: The Revolutionary War Diary of Abigail Jane Stewart, Across the Wide and Lonesome Prairie: The Oregon Trail Diary of Hattie Campbell,* and *The Great Railroad Race: The Diary of Libby West.*

Widely praised for her accurate and compelling historical fiction, she is also the author of *Earthquake at Dawn,* an American Library Association Best Book for Young Adults; and *Jenny of the Tetons,* which won a Golden Kite Award for fiction. Each book was named a New York Public Library Book for the Teen Age. All of the above titles are Notable Children's Trade Books in the Field of Social Studies.

While not writing or reading, Kristiana loves to swim, take long walks with her golden retriever, Russell, and play marathon Scrabble games with her family. She's a dreadful cook. She and her husband live in Boise, Idaho, with their two teenage sons.

DEDICATED WITH MUCH LOVE
TO MY FATHER, HAL GREGORY,
WHOSE APPRECIATION OF ANCIENT LITERATURE
GAVE ME THE COURAGE
TO PEEK AT PLUTARCH AND ALL THE REST.

Acknowledgments

Cover painting by Tim O'Brien

Page 196: Cleopatra, Corbis-Bettman, New York, New York.

Page 197 (top): Sculpted head of Cleopatra, North Wind Picture Archives, Alfred, Maine.

Page 197 (bottom): Cleopatra from temple of Dendera, North Wind Picture Archives, Alfred, Maine.

Page 198: Map of ancient Egypt, North Wind Picture Archives, Alfred, Maine.

Page 199 (top): Map of ancient city of Alexandria, North Wind Picture Archives, Alfred, Maine.

Page 199 (bottom): Map of ancient Roman Empire, Archive Photos, New York, New York.

Page 200: King Ptolemy I Soter, North Wind Picture Archives, Alfred, Maine.

Page 201: King Ptolemy XII, North Wind Picture Archives, Alfred, Maine.

Page 202 (top): Julius Caesar, North Wind Picture Archives, Alfred, Maine.

Page 202 (bottom): Marc Antony, North Wind Picture Archives, Alfred, Maine.

Page 203: Augustus Caesar, North Winds Picture Archives, Alfred, Maine.

Page 204: Cleopatra before Julius Caesar, The Granger Collection, New York, New York.

Page 205: Cleopatra receiving Marc Antony, North Wind Picture Archives, Alfred, Maine.

Page 206 (top): Cleopatra's barge, North Wind Picture Archives, Alfred Maine.

Page 206 (bottom): Battle of Actium, North Wind Picture Archives, Alfred, Maine.

Page 207: Cleopatra's death scene, The Granger collection, New York, New York.

Page 208: Great Pyramid, North Wind Picture Archives, Alfred, Maine.

Page 209: Sphinx, North Wind Picture Archives, Alfred, Maine.

Page 210: Pharos Lighthouse, North Wind Picture Archives, Alfred, Maine.

Page 211: Alexandrian Great Library, North Wind Picture Archives, Alfred, Maine.

Page 212 (top): Egyptian papyrus scroll, North Wind Picture Archives, Alfred, Maine.

Page 212 (bottom): Hieroglyphics, North Wind Picture Archives, Alfred, Maine.

Page 213: Goddess Isis, North Wind Picture Archives, Alfred, Maine.

Page 214: Egyptian headdress, Corbis-Bettman, New York, New York.

Page 215 (top): Egyptian jewelry, The Granger Collection, New York, New York.

Page 215 (bottom): Ivory game board, Archive Photos, New York, New York.